WHISKEY

Steel Patriots MC

Book Three

Mary Kennedy

III
INSATIABLE INK.

CHAPTER ONE

Wade "Whiskey" English waited his turn to appear before the military action and disciplinary review board. Seated outside the hearing room with his teammates, all silent, communicating only with a glance or hand gesture, not wanting anyone to know what they were saying, he stared up and down the hallway as if something or someone would appear to tell them this was all a sick joke.

He brushed a speck of dust from his pant leg, his uniform pressed perfectly, fit him like a glove, the golden eagle with a sword slashing upward representing him as Marine Special Forces gleaming on his chest, the ribbons and medals from his fifteen years as a Marine Sniper indicative of his success record.

Whiskey's team lead, Eric "Ghost" Stanton, was a Navy Seal, but the team was made up of various members of the Special Forces community. They were a team of elite warriors hand-selected by Ghost and the government to take on missions that regular teams couldn't—or wouldn't—take on. He closed his eyes for a moment letting out a long slow breath, trying to control the anger he knew was bubbling to the surface.

It was fucking idiotic that any of them were here in the first place. Terrorists had kidnapped, tortured, and murdered twelve little girls from a school, and they did what they were charged to do—took out the terrorists. Only problem was the morons involved at the top believed that when the girls were found dead, technically the mission was done. Whiskey and the team didn't see it that way. His own mother was a teacher and spent many summers teaching in third-world countries, helping children to grasp the importance of education even for only a few weeks.

Fans were blasting hot air downward, scattering dust along the hallways of the makeshift headquarters, but it only served to create more heat, blowing sand, and the stifling stench of men and women sweating. The doors opened and his teammate, Quincy "Zulu" Slater, stepped out with a scowl etched on his midnight black features. Whiskey looked up at the man with a half-grin. He always grinned when the gentle giant walked toward him. At six-foot-three, Whiskey was no small guy. Two hundred and twenty pounds of muscle packed on his tall frame, but Zulu was a beast.

A fellow SEAL from the same team as Ghost, he was probably the biggest SEAL Whiskey had ever known, and that was saying a lot. He stood six-foot-six in his stocking feet but had two hundred and eighty pounds of rock-solid muscle bulging from his body. The entire team was deadly, but Zulu was deadly in a completely different way. His black skin, black eyes, and bald head making him appear as Lucifer himself in the night.

"Sgt. Major English?" called the MP. Whiskey stood, straightening his uniform. Passing Zulu, he gave a short nod, barely perceptible to anyone other than the team.

Whiskey walked quietly, his posture rigid, between the rows of chairs to face the men sitting at the table on the dais at the front of the room. He gave a sharp salute and waited. He'd made his initial statement and filed the incident reports as directed. He'd told his story at least a dozen times, and yet they still wanted to question him more.

"Sgt. Major English, as you recall, I'm Admiral Crossing, and these other gentlemen and I are here to get to the bottom of what happened out there." He paused, staring at the big Marine in front of him. Whiskey stood silent. The asshole hadn't asked a question yet. He made a statement. He wants to put us through the fucking wringer? Well, two can play at that game.

"Sgt. Major?" his eyes traveled upward to stare Whiskey in the face.

"Sir?"

"Are you going to respond?" asked General Whitman.

"You didn't ask a question, sir," said Whiskey, staring straight ahead.

"Don't be obtuse, son. We want to know what happened out there. Your teammates have given us their versions. Now we'd like to hear it from you."

"I've given you my version, the true version, just like my teammates, several times, sir. We completed our mission, sirs. We were asked to find the twelve girls and kill the terrorists. We found the girls brutalized, hanging from a cliff. We cut them down, sent them back on the transport provided, and then hunted down the terrorists, killing them all. Mission complete."

Always faithful. Always forward.

Whiskey recited the MARSOC code in his head over and over again, trying to maintain the anger bubbling up inside him.

"Sgt. Major English, you were told if you found those girls dead, you were to return them for appropriate burial *with* your entire team. Instead, you decided to go rogue."

"With all due respect, sir, we did not go rogue. We followed the mission. You didn't see those girls, sir. You didn't see their abused bodies being plucked apart by buzzards. You didn't see the damage done to young bodies that should have been skipping rope or dancing to whatever the latest music is. You. Didn't. See." He almost spat the words at the table in front of him.

"Sgt. Major!" yelled Whitman.

"Whit," said Admiral Crossing, "calm down. None of us can say with certainty that we wouldn't have done the same thing, Sgt. Major. I know for damned sure I would have thought twice about it. I have only one question, Sgt. Major. Do you regret your actions?" Whiskey stared directly at each of the faces before him until they squirmed in their seats. Crossing just grinned at the big man, knowing what he was doing.

"I regret nothing, sir, absolutely nothing. If anything, I hope my actions give those parents some peace at night knowing their daughters' killers were removed from this planet."

"Thank you, Sgt. Major," said Crossing. "You can step outside and wait with your teammates while we finish with the others." Whiskey turned sharply on his heel and headed toward the door. He stopped suddenly, turning back to face the panel once more.

"One more thing, sirs," he said calmly, "before you decide to throw me and the team to the wolves, or court-martial us, or whatever it is you see fit, I would ask you this. If those had been your daughters, your children, would you have wanted us to walk away? Twelve girls – the four of you – think of it as three daughters each. Would you have wanted us to walk away?" Every man blanched at the statement, opening and closing their mouths, unsure of how to respond. Whiskey nodded.

"That's what I thought." He stepped outside, staring at his teammates. He took his seat next to Zulu and waited as the next man was called.

They could hear everything being said inside the room, and when Jack "Doc" Harris notified the members of the panel that he possessed photos of the girls, they all stirred a bit in their seats. Taking photos of prisoners, dead bodies, anything to do with a mission was strictly forbidden unless directed to do so. Doc could be placing a noose on all their necks, or he could be saving them.

Doc stepped outside the room and stared at his teammates, nodding to walk with him to the end of the hallway.

"Fucking hell, Doc, we didn't know you had photos," said Ghost.

"I know. I took them when we were cutting the girls down. Don't ask me why. I know it's a violation, but I just had this feeling, and shit for luck, it paid off."

"Well," said Razor, "I, for one, am fucking eternally grateful. They won't court-martial us with the fear of those photos becoming public. The liberals would be screaming about human rights, and the conservatives would say the killing of those men was justified. They don't want to have to argue that."

"This shit is getting fucking exhausting," said Ghost. "I'm so damned tired of having to follow rules created by men who don't do the damn job anymore, or for that matter ever did the job." They all nodded as the doors of the hearing room opened once again. The MP waved them inside.

Standing before the committee, the men all removed their hats and stood at attention.

"Gentlemen, you have presented us with a dilemma, and I won't lie. It's one I hate," said Admiral Crossing. "Your work as a unit has been indisputable, but we are getting pressures from the country's government claiming you murdered innocent men."

Whiskey started to speak, but the Admiral held up his hand.

"I didn't say I agree. However, we are tasked with making a show of, hell, I don't even know anymore. We are asking you to retire, gentlemen. If you refuse, you will be dishonorably discharged. If you take the retirement, there will be no mark on your records. It saddens me to do this, to lose some of the finest men I know, and that I know we need in our service."

It seemed like a no-brainer, but Whiskey was pissed that he was being forced out because of their fear of some shithole government.

"I accept retirement," said Whiskey.

"I accept retirement," said Doc.

"I accept retirement," said Ghost. The chorus was heard down the line. The Admiral nodded at them, handing them their papers that would tell administration they were taking retirement effective immediately.

"You will be expected to be packed and on the next transport home within forty-eight hours. I wish you good luck, men. The world needs people like you. I hope you find a way to continue the good fight."

Whiskey stared at the panel for a moment longer, wanting to unleash his anger on them. Thinking the wiser choice was simply to walk away with his honorable discharge in hand, he followed the rest of his team outside. Thirty-six hours later, they were seated on a transport discussing their futures.

"Where will you go, Ghost?" asked Whiskey. Ghost looked at the men he'd called teammates for the last decade. Each man was hand-selected for his team, partly because he knew of their skills, but mostly because he trusted them with his life and the lives of every member of the team.

"I have a proposition for all of you. I know some of you have family back home, but nobody has an old lady that I'm aware of," he said, smirking at the men on the transport.

"Well, Tango has a mule he's fond of," said Doc with a smile.

"Fuck you, Doc, at least it's a female mule," he grinned. "So, what's your point, Ghost?"

"My point is, when my pops died, he left me a huge piece of land. It's nothing special, but it's got an old garage on the property where he used to repair cars, bikes, tractors, shit like that for neighbors. The house burned down years ago, but Pops made the barn into a pretty livable space."

"Sooooo, you want us all to live there?" asked Gunner.

"No, I mean, yea. Look, I ride. You all know that, and I know that most of you do too. What if, what if we formed our own club—motorcycle club? We pick a name, make the garage something that we can all work, and maybe open a bar, or some shit."

The men all looked at one another, nodding. It was a good idea, but not one of them knew anything about running a business or a bar.

"I'm in," said Tango, "but I know jack-shit about operating a bar. I can fix anything with a motor, and so can most of you, but a bar? I don't know, man. I know *how* to drink, just not how to mix drinks."

"Look, it doesn't have to happen right away. MCs are pretty territorial. We need to make sure we're not stepping on anyone's toes. I'm not a fan of becoming an outlaw MC. We got our taste of outlaw in that fucking shithole we just came from, and it didn't do any of us any good. I'm suggesting that between the bar and the garage, we'll have two legitimate businesses. Maybe, maybe on the side, we sort of informally help people."

"Help people? Like good Samaritans?" asked Gunner.

"Sort of, I'm thinking more like we take jobs others won't, but only the ones we want to take. We find lost kids, kidnap victims. We help the old lady being screwed over by a nasty landlord, shit like that." The men all looked at him, raising their eyebrows. "Look, I know we've spent our entire careers doing just this kind of shit, but now we get to do it on our terms. The shop needs cleaning up, and the barn will need to be made inhabitable, adding more electrical, plumbing, but it's huge. I've got a shit ton of money saved from all my deployments, and Pops left me a nice little chunk of change."

"And we'd be partners?" asked Whiskey.

"Yea, we'd be fucking partners. We'd be brothers, asshole," he said with a grin. "Just like we are now. We'd rely on one another and do shit our way. No red tape, no governments telling us what to do. We ride our fucking bikes when we want; we take the jobs we want; we fuck who we want, and we drink 'til we can't drink no more." The men smiled in his direction.

"I'm in," said Tango.

"Me too," said Doc.

"Why the fuck not?" said Razor.

"Fuck, you know I'm in, asshole," said Gunner.

"I guess we need a name," said Whiskey. "How about Steel Soldiers?"

"No fucking way, asshole. I'm a SEAL, not a fucking soldier," said Tango. The others laughed and nodded. They were all from different branches of the military and loved teasing each other about the superiority of their own branch, but deep down held mad respect for one another.

"Steel Patriots," said Ghost. "The steel between our legs and the fucking patriot spirit we all still carry."

"Steel Patriots," whispered Whiskey. The others nodded and smiled.

"Steel Patriots it is."

CHAPTER TWO

Whiskey stared into his beer, thinking of the woman he'd been watching on and off for the last few weeks. Stubborn, beautiful, and completely off-limits. She was the key to getting to Krevnyv. After all, she was his only daughter. The problem was every time Whiskey thought of the young woman, he developed a raging hard-on that nothing could alleviate. He'd taken more cold showers in the last few weeks than he had since he was a teenager. He remembered every detail of their first meeting.

Ace dropped Whiskey off near Georgetown, where he made his way toward the address they had on Katarina Krevnyv. He had seen the picture, but the data confirmed that she was twenty-two, almost twenty-three with a birthday in just a few days, five-foot-six, one hundred and sixteen pounds, blonde and blue-eyed. She had an undergraduate degree in criminal justice and was nearly complete with her degree at Georgetown Law School.

The sprawling three-story Georgian townhome easily cost several million dollars, the neighborhood one of the finest in the D.C. area. Foreign cars lined the street, not a pathetic domestic brand in sight, although he had to smile at the custom-built motorcycle in the driveway of the house three over from Katarina.

He recognized every feature of the bike. The twin exhaust, custom chrome, tank with a soaring eagle on a red, white, and blue background; it was beautiful. He should know. He'd helped build that bike, and at fifty grand, it wasn't cheap.

The front door opened to a long, leggy blonde stepping onto the porch. She locked the door and made her way down the block to the train station. Interesting. Rich girl with a hot ride, and yet she takes the train.

Whiskey watched as the cascade of blonde hair swung back and forth down her back. Her tall body was lean, like that of a dancer. She wore blue jeans with a small-heeled ankle boot; he couldn't see her top with the heavy wool coat, but she carried what he knew was a very expensive designer bag.

Standing several yards away, he watched as she waited for the train. She stepped into the third car, and he took the second one, still having her in his line of sight. A few stops later, she left the train heading to street level. Whiskey kept his distance, biding his time until he could be sure she was alone. She ducked into a coffee shop, and he waited outside, casually glancing at the magazines on the rack outside.

Katarina and her coffee came out a few minutes later, and she made her way onto campus. It was pretty dead for a university campus, and then it dawned on Whiskey that it was most likely winter break. He didn't attend college in the traditional way, but he knew enough to know kids were out pretty much after the first week of December.

He watched as she entered the law library and cursed, knowing he would need a student ID to get in. A young student came toward him, precariously balancing several books, and Whiskey saw his chance, the ID hanging loosely from his pocket.

The library was a spectacular building, and on another day, he might actually enjoy exploring it. At the desk, an older woman asked for his ID.

"Chan Yun Phat?" she questioned. He shrugged his shoulders.

"Adopted." She grinned but nodded in his direction. Whiskey wound his way through the bookshelves not seeing who he was looking for. Spotting the staircase to the second level, he made his way up and started the same process of winding up and down the aisles. At the back of the stacks, he heard the noise too late as he was slammed into a rack of books. A fierce expression filled the face of Katarina Krevnyv as she reached up to hold a small knife at his throat.

"Tell my fucking father I don't need babysitters," she growled. Whiskey could only smile at the fierceness of the little lion. He had to give her credit. He outweighed her easily by a hundred pounds and had a good ten inches of height on her.

"I don't work for Daddy," he said, grinning. She shoved her forearm harder against his chest, but he could see the uncertainty in her face.

Oh hell! I am seriously outmanned with this guy, thought Kat. I can feel his muscles flexing below my arm like he's going to pounce. What the hell have I done?

"I want to speak with you about your father and his... business dealings," he said.

"I have nothing to do with my father and his business dealings," she practically spit the words at him.

"I believe you, beautiful. I just want to ask you some questions." She eyed him carefully up and down, looking around to see if there was anyone else. "You and I both know I could overpower you at any time. I'm not because I don't want to scare you or hurt you. I just want to talk to you."

Katarina seemed to be taking him in at that moment. He was so tall and muscular, his golden-brown eyes matching his hair, the sexy whiskers telling her he was no college student. This was a man. A man easily ten years her senior, if not more. She lowered the small knife and took a step back.

Whiskey then got a good view of what had been under that jacket. She wore an ivory sweater, clinging to small curves and a long torso. Her nearly white-blonde hair and blue eyes were the most beautiful combination he'd ever seen on a woman. He knew she was early twenties, but something in her eyes said she was much older.

"What do you want? Who are you?" she finally asked.

"Can we sit?" he asked.

"No." He grinned at her.

"Okay, my name is Wade English, but my friends call me Whiskey. I belong to a motorcycle club called the Steel Patriots. We help local and federal agencies find missing people, especially missing children and trafficked women."

He saw the hitch in her breath and the flicker of fear in her eyes. He started to reach for her, but she backed up, shaking her head.

"I don't know anything. Please, leave me alone."

"Katarina, you may know more than you think you do. These girls, these children, need our help. We think your father is holding them somewhere, and we need to find them. Now you're either helping us or helping your father. Which is it?"

"You know nothing of me!" she said, stabbing his chest with her finger. "I'm not helping my father. I want nothing to do with him. He's a monster!"

"Yes, he is," he said quietly. "With friends like Omar, he couldn't be classified as anything but a monster." Katarina sucked in a breath. How did he know about this? How could he know?

"I won't go. He can't make me..."

"You know that he can. He'll find a way, Kat. My men and I will protect you if you'll let us."

"Don't call me Kat. It's Katarina. I... you... you can't protect me. Don't you understand? No one can protect me. As long as I'm here at school, he won't come for me." Whiskey shook his head and reached for her hand. The long delicate fingers linked with his own.

For just a moment, just a fraction of a moment, Katarina felt safe... felt hope fill her chest, and then realized how foolish she was.

"If you let us, we can protect you. He can get to you anywhere, Kat. You know he can. He's already killed several young girls, and there are at last a dozen more out there somewhere in a truck waiting for him to deliver them to their deaths. Don't do this. Don't help him." Tears trailed down her alabaster cheeks, and she shook her head.

"I don't know anything. I don't live with him anymore, and I refuse to be involved in his activities. He's heinous, absolutely heinous. The FBI was supposed to get him out of the country after I helped them with my mother and brother. They lied! They lied to me, and now I have to tolerate his weekly dinners and visits. I have to hear him threaten me with Omar, and I won't. I refuse! I'll kill myself before I allow that man to lay a finger on me. I swear I will!"

"I believe you, beautiful," he said, letting out a long breath. "Listen, Katarina, I know you don't know me, but you can trust me. I promise you, I'm one of the good guys. I know you don't have a reason to believe that right now, but I want you to trust me when I say I won't let your father or Omar get to you if you'll just come with me and let us help you."

She shook her head, biting that lower lip.

"Who... who are you really?" she asked.

"I told you who I really am. I'm Wade "Whiskey" English. I'm retired United States Marine Corps, MARSOC sniper. I'm currently part of the Steel Patriots motorcycle club. Ask anyone... except your father," he grinned, "and they'll tell you about us. We're legitimate, Katarina."

"Why? Why would you help me?" she asked. Why indeed, thought Whiskey.

"Because I'm an idiot who can't refuse to help a beautiful woman."

Her feisty temperament turned him the fuck on! She went up against a Marine, knowing he could break her in two. All that long blonde hair, lean dancers' legs, and pert little breasts made him want to dive in face first. There were several problems, though, not the least of which

she was the daughter of a Russian crime boss who had his hands in drugs,

sex trafficking, money laundering, and God knew what else. She was

young, almost twenty years his junior. She was rich. He had nothing he

could offer her in that department, and oh, yea, she was young.

"Fuck," he muttered into his beer. Grace stared up at Whiskey

from behind the bar and smiled at him.

"Is it me, or are you just grumpy today? Actually, grumpy for the

last few weeks?" she asked, smiling at the man.

Whiskey stared at Grace and her slightly protruding belly. She

and Ghost found love in the most unconventional way when Gracie

showed up at their gates, nearly beaten to death by her ex-husband.

Ghost immediately fell in love and wouldn't let the woman out of his

sight. Now Gracie was expecting their first and most likely only child,

considering they were both in their forties. It seemed a gift from God

himself, bearing in mind her ex also killed their eighteen-year-old twin

daughters in his maniacal rampage.

"Sorry, Gracie," said Whiskey, "I don't mean to be an ass, just a lot

on my mind." She nodded and moved toward the Christmas tree that

Bree was standing next to. Aubrey, or Bree as she preferred, was the fiancé of Doc. They were a beautiful couple, and Whiskey was happy as shit that Doc found his true love. He turned, seeing Zulu walk toward him looking tired, more from lack of sleep than work.

"You okay, brother?" he asked. "You look like you haven't slept."

"Dreams, brother, fucking dreams." Zulu rubbed a huge bear-like paw over his face and groaned.

"Same one?" asked Whiskey, concerned for his teammate and brother.

"Yea, same fucking dream every time. I'm in my hospital bed at Walter Reed, and this woman with a white halo of hair around a pale face leans over me. Her eyes are glowing. I shit you not, glowing. She's whispering to me, but I can't hear anything she's saying. It's so fucking real. I reach for her every time, and then she just disappears."

"Maybe you should talk to Bree, brother," said Whiskey with concern. "I mean, it's not a nightmare, so that's good, but maybe it's something else. It doesn't sound threatening or anything."

"No, it's definitely not. It's just, fuck, brother, it's been almost fifteen years since I was in that place, and I'm still dreaming about this woman. I don't even know if she's real or made up." Whiskey nodded, watching Bree and Grace flit around the main room of the clubhouse.

They were busy decorating the club for Christmas, lights hanging everywhere, stockings on the walls, the scents of orange and cinnamon filling the air, and even Christmas music playing. The fifteen-foot spruce was standing in the corner, the smell of its needles mixing with the cinnamon and orange.

"This place looks like the fucking north pole," said Whiskey, staring at the big open space of Club Steel.

"Oh, don't be such a scrooge," said Doc, standing next to Zulu at the bar. "Grace and Bree both love Christmas, so let them have this. Besides, remember how great Thanksgiving was? Holidays with the women around seem to be getting better and better, and I, for one, appreciate it. We've never had this, all of this. Being overseas all those years, and then it just being us here for so long, it's kinda nice having a woman's touch to the holidays." Whiskey only nodded, a cynical look on his face.

"Any word from Ivan?" asked Ghost. Ivan Pechkin was their connection to Krevnyv, working undercover on his team. Ivan worked with the team in the Middle East several times, having been former SAS and now working with the FBI.

"Nothing. I'm really worried about him. He usually checks in with me every few days," said Whiskey. "If I don't hear anything in the next few days, I may have our contact at the bureau start looking for him." Ghost and Doc nodded as the front door to the club opened. A blast of cold air hit their faces, white flurries the backdrop for the woman coming toward them.

Entering through the doors, she was someone they all recognized. She was tall, blonde, blue-eyed, and currently very dirty with a black eye and split lip. She had a slight limp as she moved toward the man her eyes were locked onto.

"Fuck! Katarina!" said Whiskey, running to the young woman. He gently gripped her shoulders, turning her to face him. "Are you okay?"

She shook her head, shaking as much from the cold as her acknowledgement that she was not okay. She had on the same white sweater he'd seen her in that day at the library and only a thin jacket over that. Her hands were red and raw, her cheeks chapped and flushed from the wind.

"It… It took me a while to find you," she said, shaking. "I… I asked around and finally hitched a ride up here. The people… the people in town pointed me this way."

"Honey, come in. What happened?" he asked, seating her at a nearby table. Bree and Grace rushed to her side, grabbing a blanket and wrapping it around her shoulders. Bree set a glass of water and whiskey in front of her, and Grace rushed to pour a cup of coffee. He could already hear her directing the kitchen to bring out hot food.

"My father, he sent his men to bring me to the house. I didn't have a choice. They pulled me from my home and shoved me into the car. When I got there, Omar was there."

"Fucking hell," said Whiskey.

"He… he sold me. He sold me to that man for a million dollars," she sniffed. "My own father, my own father sold me to that man. He said it was time to pay my debt. I refused, tried to run. I kicked my father, and he punched me. Omar tried to grab my arm, and when I shoved him, he slapped me across the face and hit me again. When I was finally able to stand, I just ran. I've been running for five days. I tried to get some things from my house, but they're watching it. All I had was my backpack with a few things in it. I... you didn't give me a business card. I couldn't call you. There's no listing for the Steel Patriots, and I didn't know the name of the restaurant." Tears were streaming down her dirt-streaked face.

"It's okay, honey. You came to the right place," said Bree, hugging her shoulders.

"What do you need me to do," asked Whiskey. "Just tell me. Anything." She swallowed, taking a sip of the whiskey sitting in front of her.

"I need you to kill my father... and Khanaman Omar."

CHAPTER THREE

"Did she just ask you to kill her father?" asked a wide-eyed Zulu. Katarina looked toward the booming rumble of the man's voice, her gaze gliding up, up, up to see his face. He was one of the biggest men she'd ever met, and that was saying something considering her father's team of Russian goons.

"I-I did ask that. And Omar, they both have to die." She looked around the table at the raised eyebrows.

"Honey, we get that him selling you is shitty, and we can help you with getting away," said Whiskey, "but we don't murder people just because we don't like what they do." Katarina pulled out her phone and turned it on, flipping open the photo app. She handed the phone to Whiskey and watched as he and Ghost scrolled through the photos.

"I don't think," Alex "Ace" Mills was their tech and comms guy, standing off to the side he was going to warn her about the possibility of them tracking her phone when she spoke.

"I've turned off the tracking and location service," she said with a small smile. "I had it off to preserve the battery. I took these photos a few days before my father took me. It might be why he finally sold me. I don't know. I'm forced to do weekly dinners with my father, and I do mean forced. I hate them. I mean, literally, physically hate him! But if I don't go, the punishments can be brutal." She swallowed and looked up at the concerned faces in front of her. Doc knelt beside the young woman, his small emergency kit in his hands.

"Sorry," said Doc, "before we continue, I just want to be sure you don't have any pressing medical needs. I'm going to check your vitals, and you can keep talking. First, though, are you hurt anywhere other than the bruises on your face? Any cuts? Potential broken bones?" She smiled at the tall man shaking her head.

"No, no, I'm fine other than the obvious and being cold, dirty, and hungry. I have a bad blister on my left heel, but nothing a bandage wouldn't help." He nodded, smiling at her and then at the pretty redhead next to her. They must be a couple, thought Kat.

"My father hates me, and I'm not exaggerating in that. He truly despises me. I'm certain he knows that I was the one who fed information to the FBI that got my mother and brother killed. They were selling children on the black market. I had no choice. No choice. It sickened me. It was purely accidental that I found out, but when I did, I was able to get the information to them. I've been working with Ivan since then. I know you know him. He told me I could trust you after that day you approached me at the university. I-I asked him." Whiskey just nodded and smiled.

"The photos?" asked Ace.

"Yes, well, my father forced me to have one of our dinners a few nights before all this happened. He was distracted more than usual, and men kept running in, interrupting our dinner to tell him things. I couldn't hear what was being discussed, but at one point, he excused himself. There was all this noise coming from the hallway leading to the basement. He was gone a long time, so I decided to follow the noise I was hearing... all the commotion." She took a deep breath as if steeling herself for what she had to say.

"I followed the noise, and it led directly to the basement. I never go down there. I know it's silly, but I don't like basements. I don't like dark spaces," she said, smiling at the group of people. For the first time, she noticed the two women were sitting next to her, rubbing her hand and arm in a comforting gesture. She smiled at them, silently thanking them for the courage to continue.

"I could hear crying. At first, it just sounded like one person, a woman, but then it was more. I was as quiet as I could be making my way down the stairs. I used to be a dancer, a ballerina, so I know how to step quietly when I need to, gently. Anyway, as I got further and further downstairs, I noticed two large doors that led out toward the back driveway were open. I've never noticed those doors before, but women were being led down through those doors."

"They... they were barely dressed. Some only had on bra and panties, but worse than that, they weren't really women at all. They were all younger than me, maybe teenagers. One, one was definitely only a child, maybe eight or nine. The men were my father's men," she swallowed the bile rising in her throat.

"Take your time, honey," said Whiskey, staring into her blue eyes.

"His men were grabbing them, touching them intimately." She blushed a hot pink on her cheeks and heard the rumbling curses of the men around her. "One of my father's men, Dolf, he's brutal, cruel in fact, and enjoys it. He... h-he said the men were to train the women for Omar, that he was taking all of them, but wanted them, oh God. The men started to rape the women one by one, moving from one woman to the next." Her sobs came harder now, thinking of what those poor women were being put through.

"I made my way back upstairs as quickly as I could. I turned the corner of the dining room, and my father and one of his men were sitting there waiting for me. When he asked me where I was, I said I had gone to the restroom. I was shaking so bad I know he didn't believe me. All I could think about was getting the information to Ivan and getting the hell out of my father's home. My father got up and said he was going to have to cut the dinner short. He had *business* to attend to."

"I was relieved. I was shaking so badly I didn't think I could continue, but then he said I needed to get ready to meet Omar later in the week, that it was time to meet my future husband. I told him I wouldn't, that I would refuse. He slapped me and told me to stop acting like a child." She shook her head, wiping the tears away with a dirty hand. "I'm telling you right now. I will not go to that man. I refuse. I will kill myself first."

"I don't think we need to go to such drastic measures," said Whiskey, reaching for her hand. "We'll find out what's going on. Did you get in touch with Ivan?"

"Y-yes, Ivan said they were aware the women had been sold to my father and were headed to Omar. He assured me that they would do everything they could to get the women out. When I asked why he didn't just raid the house, he said they wanted to cut the head off the snake." The men nodded, understanding what Ivan was saying.

"Kat," said Whiskey, knowing he was using the name she told him not to, "why don't you let Bree and Grace get you upstairs where you can shower and get some clean clothes? The building is secure. The restaurant is open to the public, but private residences are secured behind those steel doors. You're free to walk around the property. No one will get to you here. We'll talk about our next steps, and then you can come back down and get some food in you." She nodded, staring at the table.

"C-can I ask your names?" she asked, looking at the table.

"Sure, honey," said Whiskey, feeling the stares of his teammates as he said the term of endearment. "That's Doc, Ace, Ghost, Zulu, Grace, Bree, and then behind you is Tango, Gunner, and Alpha. We have a few more around here, but we'll get to them later." Kat turned to see the wall of men surrounding her and smiled a nervous smile. She hadn't even heard them approach from behind.

It's a wonder you're not dead, Katarina! She chided herself.

"Thank you. Thank you all so much. I've been so scared, so... so worried about what will happen. When Wade, umm, Whiskey approached me at the university, I didn't know if I could trust him. I'm sorry I didn't sooner."

"Don't worry about it, Katarina," said Ghost. "We're going to do everything we can to help you." She nodded, following Grace and Bree through the double steel doors and up the stairs. Ghost waited, watching the three women make their way through the restaurant and toward their private quarters. When the women were gone, he turned to the group of men.

"Fucking son-of-a-bitching hell!"

CHAPTER FOUR

While Kat showered in the room that once belonged to Grace, Bree went in search of some clean things for her to wear. Since the Steel Patriots were involved in recovering a lot of women involved in kidnappings or human trafficking, Bree and Grace started a closet for the rescues filled with packages of clean underwear, bras of varying sizes, jeans, sweatpants, sweaters, sweatshirts, and t-shirts and even several different sizes of plain white canvas tennis shoes.

There were also small care packages of toiletries. Shampoo, conditioner, toothbrush, toothpaste, deodorant, lotions, feminine products, and even makeup and small vials of fragrance.

By the time Kat stepped from the bathroom, she looked like a completely different woman. Her long blonde hair was coiled in a tight bun at the nape of her neck, the blue jeans were a little loose on her thin frame, but they showed her curves perfectly. The crewneck sweater was a soft shade of gray, making her eyes appear more gray than blue.

Free of the dirt, her porcelain skin glowed in the afternoon light. If it weren't for the bruises and fading black eye, she would be positively stunning.

"You look beautiful, honey," said Grace. Kat gave a small smile, looking at the women who waited patiently for her on the bed.

"I can't thank you all enough for this," she said, waving her hand at the clothing. "I just had nowhere to go, no other family to take me in."

"Well, you have somewhere now," said Bree. "Like Whiskey said, the residences are behind a steel gate and the two steel doors you saw. The bike shop is at the front of the property, and you're welcome to visit, just don't go outside the fence line. Everything is secure here, top-notch cameras and sensors. Also, I'm a licensed therapist as well, Kat, so if you want to talk about anything, I'm here for you."

"Oh, oh, I might. I mean," she pulled her bottom lip between her teeth and sat in the overstuffed chair behind her. Tears filled her eyes, and Grace moved to kneel in front of her.

"It's okay, honey. It's all going to be okay. You'll see. The boys will take care of this." Kat shook her head.

"It won't ever be okay. I'm so fucked up. My family is so fucked up! God, I'm a mess!" she said, wiping the tears away. "First, my mother and brother are selling babies on the black market, and now my father is trafficking women to that monster, Omar! Jesus, what does that make me?! What kind of person does that make me?"

"It makes you brave for running," said Bree. "Honey, we don't get to choose our biological family. But the Steel Patriots give us all a chance to choose our preferred family."

"Oh," said Kat quietly. She thought of the sexy man downstairs with the eyes matching his name. Whiskey was much older than her; she knew that, but he made her feel things she'd never felt before. "I-I don't know. I tried to get away, you know, many times. I moved to New York once, and my father simply made a few calls, and one of the other crime families found me, turning me over to his men. While I was on tour with the ballet company, I tried to escape in London. Same thing, a few days later, my father's men picked me up. I was prepared to run again this time. I'd bought a box of black hair dye, colored contacts, everything to change my appearance. I just didn't get the chance to."

"Well, you'll have plenty of time to think about what to do now. You're not going anywhere, sweetie," said Grace. "Now, we have an entire restaurant and club to decorate for Christmas. You wanna help?"

"Yes," said Kat, smiling at the women. "I'd love to. Christmas was always my favorite time of year. I used to dance the Nutcracker every year. It was my favorite dance to perform."

"That's right," said Grace, "Whiskey mentioned that you're a ballerina."

"Was... was a ballerina," said Kat. "I was a principal with the D.C. Ballet Theater, but I had to leave." She looked away and then absently rubbed her leg.

"Were you injured?" asked Grace with a concerned, motherly expression.

"You might say that," she said with disdain. "My father... my father said I needed to stop dancing and focus on my *job* of becoming a good wife for Omar. When I refused, he took my decision from me. I was mugged and robbed in an alley coming from the theater. Both of my legs were broken—intentionally. Nothing else was touched—not my face, not my arms, nothing—just my legs. Although they're healed, I'll never be able to sustain the positions the way I did before. Now I just dance for myself to keep my soul alive."

"Jesus," whispered Bree. "I'm so sorry, honey. So, so sorry." Kat nodded and stood once more.

"Do you think I could get some food?" she asked shyly. Both women smiled at her, nodding.

"That we can do, honey! George is the best chef in the world!" As Kat followed the women down the long hallways toward the first of the steel doors, she couldn't help but wonder if this was where she was meant to be. Maybe this is a beginning. Maybe...

CHAPTER FIVE

"Well, this is rightly fucked up," said Whiskey. "I think we all know that we have to kill Krevnyv and Omar." Ghost's eyebrows rose in a surprised expression.

"What?" asked Zulu, staring at Ghost. "You don't think we should kill this bastard?"

"No, I mean, yea, I do. I just think we have to be sure of what we're doing here. Killing Krevnyv or even Omar isn't the issue. It's the after shit we need to be careful of."

"What the fuck are you talking about, Ghost?" asked Whiskey. "You suddenly becoming concerned with what happens after we kill because you got a woman and baby on the way?"

"Don't fucking speak to me that way, Whiskey," he growled, standing to his full height of six-foot-four. "We're brothers, always brothers, but don't speak of my wife and child like that."

"I'm sorry. You're right. This is just fucked up, brother," Whiskey said apologetically.

"I know. Listen, I want to put a bullet in both their brains, easy thing to do. But Krevnyv runs the Russian mafia here and in Russia, as well as ties to the other major ethnic crime families in the U.S. Killing him could bring every mafia family on the planet down on us. That kind of mess we don't need tracked back to us. And Omar? That fucker has diplomatic immunity. Even if we caught him red-handed, he could easily get out of whatever shit we find him in."

"Ghost is right," said Ace. "This has to be handled delicately, which is why I've had a trace on their laptops and phones for the last two weeks." Ghost looked up again with the arched eyebrow. The other men all turned to stare at Ace.

Alex "Ace" Mills was a thirty-four-year-old bona fide genius. His IQ put every one of them to shame, hovering over the 150 mark. At six-foot even, he was one of the smaller men on the team. His lean muscles were more like a distance runner or swimmer, but make no mistake, Navy Intelligence trained him to be the best, and he was fucking deadly.

"You put a trace on their computers and phones? How? I mean, I know how, but how did you get access to them?" asked Whiskey.

"Krevnyv had been sending messages to Mabel about the girls we found in Toronto. I was able to track his IP address and enter through a backdoor, so to speak. Once I did that, I was able to find communications between him and Omar." Ace just stared at them as if it weren't the most amazing thing ever.

"Okay, and what have you found?" asked Ghost in awe of the younger man.

"They're both nervous for different reasons. As of an hour ago, when I checked after Sunshine walked in the door," he stared at Whiskey with a half-grin, "daddy-dearest has every goon on the planet searching for his daughter with a bounty of one million. Omar is threatening to not only kill him but sabotage his relationships with the Russian mob families and the other families as well. They have men at her townhouse literally sitting there waiting for her to return; the university is covered, and now they are scouring travel manifests for flights, trains, rental car companies—anything."

"Any reason for them to think she might be here?" asked Zulu.

"No, there was video in the Georgetown library, but I hacked in and erased the entire day that Whiskey and her met. Here's the thing.

Omar paid the million to Krevnyv for his daughter, but he promised him another five million if he'd deliver a dozen girls to him by the end of the month."

"The girls Kat saw in the basement?" asked Whiskey.

"That would be my guess, but the problem is those girls disappeared mysteriously." Ace looked at the table of men.

"Ivan."

"Ivan," said Ace. "My guess is he disrupted the shipment at the docks somehow. They were scheduled to leave on a freighter three days ago. The freighter is still sitting there, and if they had their cargo, they would have been long gone."

"But no sign of Ivan?" asked Ghost.

"Nothing yet. He may be in hiding now. With the disappearance of Kat and now the girls, Krevnyv is going to suspect Ivan for sure. I'll let you know if I hear any other chatter." Ace turned to walk back toward his 'room of solitude' as he liked to refer to it.

"Ace!" yelled Whiskey. He turned to look at his brother. "Great fucking work, brother." Ace nodded, a small grin slipping from his otherwise stoic features.

"Alright," said Ghost. "Number one priority is keeping Kat safe until we can find out where her father and Omar are. Whiskey? Can I assume you'll want to keep the tiny dancer close?" Whiskey sneered at his friend and heard the soft snickers of his teammates.

"Fuck all of you! She's just a kid," he growled.

"She may be a kid in age to you, brother, but she's a grown-ass woman with a body and brain to boot. She doesn't look at you like a father-figure, Whiskey. You need to re-evaluate," smiled Zulu.

"It doesn't matter. I'm almost twenty fucking years older than her! She's just a fucking child. I'll keep her safe, but that's all."

"I'm not a child," said Kat quietly from behind them.

Whiskey turned, his breath catching in his chest causing a sharp pain straight to his heart, seeing the hurt in her beautiful eyes. Staring at the now clean face of Kat, he could hardly breathe. Her body hugged in denim, the curve of her breasts filling out the soft gray sweater.

"I'm not a child. I don't have the brain or body of a child. I have more experience in this world than women three times my age. I may need you to protect me, but don't you dare assume what I need beyond that. I've had enough men in my life forcing me to do shit I don't want to do. Newsflash, asshole! I'm a woman—full grown." She spread her arms out to emphasize the point.

"I have a law degree as of just a few weeks ago. I'm an accomplished dancer. I'm well-read, and although I may not have fought in war zones, I've visited a few. So, get this straight, buddy," she said, pointing a finger at Whiskey's chest. "I don't need your alpha-male bullshit, so don't do me any favors by thinking giving me your body is some consolation prize. I. Don't. Need. It." She turned on her heels and moved toward the bar where a plate of stew and a sandwich waited for her.

The men all flushed and looked down at their feet as Bree and Grace glared at them.

"You're all idiots," said Grace.

"Amen," agreed Bree as they followed Kat.

"Well, fuck me!" mumbled Whiskey.

CHAPTER SIX

Kat's hands were shaking by the time she reached the barstool. She hadn't meant to lose her temper. She was tired, hungry, and seriously done with the bullshit the men in her life created for her. Trying to push it from her mind, she focused on the food in front of her.

The hot stew smelled heavenly, and as she took a careful bite, she felt the sting of unwanted tears fill her eyes. When she saw Whiskey, and his face lit up as she walked in the door, she'd believed that he felt something for her beyond protective instincts, but that certainly didn't come through in his words with his teammates. Maybe she'd been mistaken. What a joke! Why would he feel anything for her?

Remembering the day in the library, she felt the warmth pooling between her legs at just one look of the man. He was all hard, rigid muscle. His whiskey-colored eyes staring down at her made her melt. He'd been so kind and gentle. Now, he thought of her as a child. She had no clue how old Whiskey was, but she knew he was considerably older than her twenty-three years. But age truly was just a number. She might be twenty-three, but she'd lived through more hell than men or women twice her age.

She wasn't lying when she'd said she'd traveled to war zones. Bosnia, Herzegovina, Croatia, Afghanistan, always with her parents. They were always off conducting some sort of business, most likely illicit business, but Kat made sure that she went out to visit the people who were suffering, bringing food and blankets, anything to help them.

She'd survived university as a sixteen-year-old, grossly out of place amongst her fellow students, and finished her law degree just recently. Most thought she was still an undergraduate student, but they had no clue that she started school so early. Men noticed her all the time for all the wrong reasons—her face, her hair, her legs as a dancer. Now the one man she'd hoped would notice her for all the right reasons thought of her as nothing but a child.

"You okay, honey?" asked Grace, gently rubbing her arm.

"I will be," she said, sniffling as she took another bite of stew. "It's stupid. I'm stupid!"

"You're not stupid, honey," said Bree. "Men are stupid. All of them! Sometimes, they just need a good swift kick in the, well, a good swift kick." Kat chuckled at the beautiful redhead.

"I just thought… I thought he cared. I thought he felt something for me."

"He does. I do," said the deep voice of Whiskey from behind her. Kat stopped with the spoon halfway to her mouth. Bree and Grace smiled at her, stepping off the stools and moving to the other side of the room. "I do feel something, Kat."

"You said… you said I was a child," she said, looking directly at him. He gripped her knees, turning her to face him. His thick thighs trapping her legs between them, although if she got pissed at him, his dick was gonna get both knees slammed into it.

"I didn't mean it like that, Kat," he said, brushing a strand of hair from her face. "Listen, honey, I haven't had a woman in my life in a long time. I'm a bit rusty here."

"You mean," she looked at him questioningly.

"I don't mean I've been a monk. I just mean I haven't had anyone steady in my life in years." She nodded and blushed, looking up at him. "Listen, baby, I'm forty-one years old. Retired Marine. I spend a lot of time here at the club, but I do own my own home. I drive a truck that's six years old, a motorcycle that's currently my one and only true love. I'm

not a millionaire. I don't know that I can give you the life you deserve."
He smiled at her and was grateful for the beautiful smile she flashed back.

"I knew you were older, Whiskey. That doesn't matter to me. You know enough about me to know that my twenty-three years isn't the same as others. I've experienced more in my life than most people. Our age difference is eighteen years. So what? Who cares? Please don't make assumptions about the type of life I deserve. What I want is a normal life. I don't need or want fancy cars or handbags or homes. Those were things my father wanted. I want a normal life. One without the Russian mafia or drugs or human trafficking. I want a normal life with a normal career and a man who wants the same things and wants me. I don't know what will happen with us, but I know that you're the first man I've ever completely trusted, ever."

"Baby, that means a lot. Really, it does." He reached up and cupped her soft cheek, his rough thumb pad gliding over the fading bruise.

"And," she said, looking up at him with lust-filled eyes, her cheeks burning with embarrassment, "you're the only man I've ever had thoughts of being intimate with." Whiskey smiled down at her, and then the weight of her words hit him. She was a virgin. A fucking virgin!

"You... you've never been with a man?" asked Whiskey quietly. She shook her head. "Baby, I... I'm honored that you would want to be with me, but..."

"But what? Don't insult me, Whiskey. Don't insult what I know I want. I know what I'm asking, Whiskey. I know this is nothing right now, nothing except desire, and I hope friendship. It might never be anything more. I know you can't promise me tomorrow. Hell, I can't promise you tomorrow! What I do know is I want to spend time with you. I want to be near you. I want to experience everything you have to offer, Whiskey— everything—and not just as my protector."

"Fucking hell, baby," he said, swallowing. The sharp Adam's apple bobbed up and down as he swallowed, and Kat thought it was the sexiest thing she'd ever seen in her life. She turned slightly and took another bite of stew.

"I'll be here, Whiskey, waiting for you." She turned back to her food and focused on filling her empty stomach because if she didn't, she would surely focus on her cracking heart. Whiskey continued to sit next to her as she ate her meal, staring at her, making her want to squirm in her seat. As she took the last bite of food, he pushed the plate from her and grabbed her hand, pulling her to follow him.

"Wh-where are we going?" she asked.

"To do something either incredibly stupid or fucking life-altering."

CHAPTER SEVEN

Whiskey opened the door to the room he used when at the club. His home was on club property, something all of the brothers were slowly doing, but they also had rooms on-property if needed. Ghost's father left him with more than two hundred acres of land that they were slowly converting into residences for the brothers and their soon-to-be families.

He opened the door to the two-room suite and shut it, locking it behind Kat. The main room had a sofa facing a big-screen television, a leather recliner to the side. In the other room was his bedroom – a room no woman ever entered. If he ever wanted a quick fuck with one of the party girls, they used the common rooms downstairs. They weren't a one-percenter club with club whores, but some of the girls from town thought they were and still showed up every Friday and Saturday night hoping for one of the brothers to own them. This room was his and only his – until now.

The king-sized bed took up most of the space, with a large master bathroom to the side. He pulled Kat toward the bed and sat at the end.

"I won't hurt you, Kat," he said quietly.

"I know that," she smiled. "I wouldn't be up here with you if I thought you were going to hurt me."

"You're so fucking beautiful, Kat. I'm just some broken down Marine with battle scars and wrinkles."

"Don't... don't do that," she said, touching his face with her tiny hand. "You're brave and smart and handsome, so very, very handsome. Every scar tells of your bravery, every wrinkle a line in the story of your life. I love every one of them. I've never, never in my entire life, wanted to be with a man the way I want to be with you, Whiskey. I knew it from the moment my hand touched you in that library. I knew I was sunk." She smiled at him, and he smiled back.

"Same, baby," he said, touching her hand against his cheek. "Why? Why are you still a virgin, Kat?"

"I just never met anyone I wanted to be with in that way... in this way. I mean, when I was dancing, a lot of the male dancers were gay or bi-sexual, which is fine, but I don't share well," she grinned at him.

"Good to know, baby, because neither do I."

"Then in college, well, at first, I was so young, and then my father's men followed me everywhere. No one could get close to me.

When I figured out they were trying to keep me a virgin for Omar, I knew I'd never meet anyone." Whiskey frowned at her statement. His head tumbling with thoughts.

"Is that why you're doing this, baby? Because you don't want Omar to have you?"

"No! God, no! Whiskey, that's not it at all. If that were true, I could have chosen a dozen other guys at Georgetown. Listen, Omar is a sick fuck, no doubt, but he would want me with or without my virginity. Although I'm sure he'd want a partial refund from my father if he thought I wasn't a virgin. That's not it at all. I don't care about Omar or what he wants. I care about you, Whiskey." She leaned forward, brushing her soft, luscious lips against Whiskey's. Feeling braver, she scooted closer, wrapping her arms around his neck, tilting her head to the side; she slid her tongue along the seam of his lips and moaned.

Whiskey gripped her waist tightly, his fingers almost touching around the tiny expanse. She was fucking everything he'd ever wanted. Suddenly the concerns of their age difference flew out of his head, and all he could think about was the woman in his arms. Pushing her back to the mattress, he ran a hand down her side, his thumb brushing against her taut nipple. Kat moaned, her hot breath against his lips.

She felt the steel rod pressing against her thigh and honestly thought she might cum just from the feel of him against her body. Gliding her hand beneath his t-shirt, she felt the ripple of his muscles and groaned against his mouth.

"Baby girl, you keep moaning like that, and I'm gonna cum in my jeans," he growled. She giggled and kissed him again.

"Your body is so beautiful," she said, feeling his chest. She pushed the t-shirt over his head and stared at the tanned skin, scars marring his chest.

"My body? Baby, you need to look in the mirror. Fuck, Kat, I'm so fucking hard for you right now, baby." He pulled the sweater over her head, unhooking the bra, tossing both to the floor. Her breasts were larger than he originally thought, the large pink nipples hard, begging for his tongue. He sucked one between his teeth and bit down gently.

"Ohhhh, oh, wow, Whiskey, that feels so good. More, please more..." He quickly unzipped her jeans, shoving them to the floor, at the same time removing her shoes. Kneeling in front of her, he pushed her thighs apart, staring at the bare pussy, glistening with desire.

"I'm gonna get you ready, baby. I need to taste you. I need to have you like this first." He ran a finger between her lips and slid in her channel. The tightness of her forcing his cock to press against the zipper of his jeans painfully. "Fuck! Baby, you're so fucking tight."

She could only nod, moaning as he ran his tongue along her slit. She could feel the hot breath against her skin, arching. He pushed her thighs further apart, amazed at how easily they lay flat against the mattress.

"Fucking hell, you're so flexible, baby..." She grinned, and taking her legs in her hands, she let them slide completely wide, sitting on the edge of the bed with her legs in a split, wide open, and bare for him. "Holy... fucking... shit! You're fucking killing me, baby."

Whiskey slid his tongue inside her again, tasting the sweet juices of his little virgin, burying his face in her as she spread wide open for him.

"Oh, oh, God, Whiskey, something's happening... something... ohhhhhhh!" He smiled up at her as her desire coated his lips.

"That's right, baby. Now you're ready for me." He stood and lowered his jeans, his throbbing cock bouncing free. The big purple head looked painful as Kat touched her fingers against it delicately. Feeling the wetness on the tip, she bravely flicked her tongue across it.

"Fuck, baby," she smiled, realizing he liked that, and opened her mouth to taste him as he had done with her. "Careful of the teeth, baby." He smiled down at her as she nodded. If he let her continue, he was going to blow. Reluctantly pulling free from between her lips, he lifted her beneath her arms and pushed her back against the pillows. Pulling out a condom from the nightstand, she frowned.

"I... I've never been with anyone. I know I have no diseases, and I'm on birth control for female issues. I'd like to feel just you," she said innocently.

"Fucking hell, woman. Yea, yea, we can do that. I've never gone bare with anyone. You're the first, baby, and I know I'm clean." She smiled, nodding at him. He pushed her legs apart again and centered himself at her entrance. Sliding his fingers inside her again, he stretched her as she looked down. Her flexibility was a fucking turn-on! She could bend her body in ways he'd never known were possible.

"Will... will that fit?" she asked, staring at his thick cock.

"It will be tight, baby girl. It will sting at first, but I promise not to hurt you," he said. She nodded, waiting for him. Clenching his jaw, he touched her entrance and wanted nothing more than to pound inside her tight pussy. He restrained himself, gently pushing a little a time. Her moans weren't helping him. She sounded like a fucking phone sex operator.

"Oh... oh wow... Whiskey, that feels... I feel so full... that's so... please..." Whiskey pushed past her barrier and stilled, hearing the sharp intake of her breath.

"It's done, baby. Just relax. It will subside," he said, kissing the side of her face. She held his face in her hands and turned him to face her, staring into his eyes. Kat kissed him passionately, sliding her tongue in and out, tasting this man who owned her body.

"You're so sexy, Whiskey, so handsome," she whispered.

"Fuck, baby girl, you're the most beautiful thing I've ever seen. You're mine, Kat. Fucking mine! You understand me?" he growled as he started to move inside her.

"Yea... yours... all yours... make me yours..." she said, wrapping her long legs around his waist. She hooked her ankles together and lifted her hips against him. "Whiskey, oh my God, I think..."

"That's right, baby... cum again for me... do it, baby... I'm barely holding on..." Whiskey felt her pussy contract around his dick, squeezing the life out of it, literally, and he let loose inside her. Growling with relief, she kissed his chest, neck, and throat, then devoured his mouth with her own.

"That was beautiful, Whiskey," she said breathlessly. "Everything I ever dreamed it would be. Thank you."

"Don't thank me, baby girl. Did you hear what I said? You're mine now, Kat. Mine. That means I'm yours too. No one will come between us. You hear me?" She nodded, kissing him again as he pulled his still hard cock from her body. He stepped into the bathroom and returned with a warm rag. Looking at his cock covered with her blood, he groaned with need once more.

Settle down, asshole. She's sore.

He wiped between her thighs and cleaned her pretty pussy, wiping away his load. Pulling back the covers, they settled beneath the sheets as she curled her body around his. Kissing her temples, he smiled to himself, feeling better than he had in years.

"It's late, baby girl. Get some sleep. Tomorrow we move your shit in here with me," he said, kissing her.

"We're staying here?" she asked.

"For now," he said, nodding. "When we know shit is settled with your father and Omar, we'll move to my house out back. Until then, we've got thirty brothers living nearby who will make sure everything is good." She nodded, kissing him again. Her small hand was gliding down his chest, his abdomen, finding the stiff cock she was seeking.

"Baby girl, you're sore," he gasped as she gripped it.

"I am," she said, smiling, "but I've been wanting to do something since I met you." He watched as the mass of blonde hair trailed down his body, her mouth opening wide as she took his entire cock in her mouth.

"Fucking life-altering."

CHAPTER EIGHT

"Where is my future wife?" asked Omar, staring at the man seated across from him. He despised dealing with the criminal. He was beneath him. The only reason he continued the relationship was to get the girls he needed for his own venture and, of course, to get his hands on his future wife. In fairness, he could get the girls from a variety of sources, but with Katarina in the deal, he continued business with Anton Krevnyv. Although right now, he was feeling no need to continue with the man other than to get his hands on his wife.

"My Katarina is a stubborn girl, Omar. You should know that before you marry her. She's run off, and we'll find her like we always do. When we get her this time, we'll turn her over to you, and you can punish her as you see fit."

"No worries about that," said Omar, grinning. "I have some particularly arousing punishments in mind for her. Although I'm curious, my Russian friend. Why do you so agreeably give up your own flesh and blood?" Krevnyv looked at the other man for a moment, prepared to give him a standard bullshit line. Instead, he opted for the truth.

"Alas, my friend, she is my blood, but not of my flesh. She is my brother's spawn, not mine." Omar raised an eyebrow at the honesty of the man. He'd suspected that perhaps she was the child of an illicit affair, but never this.

"Your brother? He's been dead a long time, my friend."

"Yes, he was killed in war. He didn't know his slut of a wife was pregnant at the time. She was a tasty morsel while he was gone," he grinned at Omar. "She was a good fuck with that big pregnant belly of hers. I paid for everything for her while he was away. When Katarina was born, she had a nervous breakdown and then suffered a second one when the news came that my brother was dead. The trauma resulted in her death. As Katarina's only living relative, I took her in to be cared for as my own."

"How very gracious of you," smiled Omar. Everything was making sense now. He had no love for the girl. She was a pawn in his little game.

"It was extremely gracious of me considering what she did to my son and wife." He growled at the other man's smiling face. "Although I suppose I should thank her for ridding me of Valentina. That bitch was not worth the trouble. The only thing good she gave me was my son, and now he's gone as well."

"Why did you keep her around for so long?"

"Entertainment," he grinned. "It was a fabulous game to watch her jump through hoops to keep her blessed freedom. Then when you so graciously offered to take her off my hands, I knew that I had made the right decision."

"Yes, well, that remains to be seen since she cannot be found," said Omar. "You see, I have my men searching for her as well, and she is nowhere to be found, my friend. Nowhere. You have four days. Four days to return her to me. If she is damaged in any way, if she is no longer a virgin, I will have my money refunded to me immediately, and then I will kill her in front of you."

"Four days is not enough time," said Anton, feeling slightly panicked. "I'll need to expand the search radius."

Omar stood, his two bodyguards close behind him. A young woman knelt beside him, the tiny scraps of her bra and panties barely covering her. A red collar circled her neck, attached to a leash in his hand. He jerked hard, and she coughed, choking at the motion.

"I see you have a new pet," said Anton, grinning at the man. His lust-filled eyes taking in the young woman. Omar reached out and stroked the brunette's head.

"Yes, she's a lovely thing. She has the ability to suck a cock better than anyone I've ever had before."

"Really?" questioned Anton, suddenly feeling his cock jump to life. Omar knew the man was waiting for an invitation. It was his style to play with the women but also with those he did business with. Omar would give him a taste of his own medicine.

"Would you like to see her in action?" asked Omar. Anton nearly choked at the desire creeping into his body. "Please have a seat." Anton sat back on the sofa, readying himself for the little pet to crawl between his thighs. Instead, Omar nodded to his guard. The big Arab unzipped his pants and gripped the girl's hair, pulling her toward him.

The look on Anton's face was priceless. Disappointment filled his body as his own cock deflated. The big Arab's cock was long and thick, surrounded by black curls. The young woman stood on her knees and began licking and sucking the man as he fucked her lips. She gagged as his length hit the back of her mouth, and Omar yanked on her chain, warning her not to gag again. She could only nod.

"Does it feel good, Arif?" he asked the bodyguard.

"It does, sir. She's very good," he said in a breathy voice.

"Take all of him, pet," he said to the woman. She nodded, continuing to suck him. "Are you close, Arif?" he asked. The man nodded, and Omar pulled the woman back as she landed on the cold tile floor.

"Fuck her, Arif, hard. She deserves it hard," he said, smiling. Arif lifted the woman from the floor easily and spread her legs wide as he wrapped her around his engorged cock. He slammed into her and admired the way she held in her gasps of pain. He was big, but this young thing was small, very small, and it made him harder.

Arif wasn't into having sex in front of others, but Omar liked watching him fuck the girls. It was fine with him, at least with this one. He had a big cock made for pleasure, and once the girls were broken, it was nice to get some relief. He wasn't into pain, but he would give pleasure if he was directed to do so.

But this little pet was different. She was tight and had big tits that bounced as he took her. He could tell she liked it rough, and he slammed her into the wall, his big hand encircling her throat. He leaned down and bit hard into the flesh of her breast. Turning, he saw the twisted fuck Anton rubbing his own crotch.

"Ready for me, pet?" he said, smiling down at the woman.

"Yes, sir," she whispered. He let her slide to the floor and pumped his cock toward her face. She knew what to do, reaching up and pulling gently on his balls, sliding a finger behind them toward his anus. He moaned as his release spewed all over her face, her tongue trying to lap up as much as she could.

Anton was hard as a rock. When he looked at Omar, he noticed the man wasn't hard at all. In fact, he watched with indifference. As if he were bored to death. Maybe he couldn't get hard?

"Clean her up for me, Arif," he said to the man as he tucked his cock inside his pants.

"Of course, sir." He pulled the woman from the floor and walked her to the bathroom. Closing the door behind them, he leaned down and kissed her hard, gripping her tit with force. She knew she couldn't make any noise or Omar would come in. "You were fucking amazing."

"So were you," she whispered. "I want you again."

"I know, my pet," He said against her lips. "We'll have time tonight when he's gone. You're mine, pet. I will get you away from him soon, even if I have to buy you for myself. Did he hurt you last night?" He'd noticed the red welts on her back earlier but said nothing.

"No," she whispered. "He just gets angry because he can't, you know, do anything. It's okay." A knock at the door jolted them back to reality.

"Arif? Take pet back to the hotel. I'm leaving with Krevnyv."

"Yes, sir," he said, smiling down at the little woman. He heard the door to Krevnyv's mansion open and close. Unzipping his pants, he buried his cock inside the little pet once more.

"I have to have you, pet. You're mine." He fucked her twice in the tiny hall bathroom and then carried her to the car, taking her back to the hotel. In the hotel room, with no one around, they made love again and again, both exhausted. She rose to wash herself in the shower before

Omar returned. Taking her position on the cushion on the floor, she appeared once again as the docile pet, her collar secure around her neck.

Arif bent down and kissed her.

"Soon, pet, soon."

CHAPTER NINE

Whiskey opened his eyes to see a mass of blonde hair spread across his chest, a tiny hand lying on his abdomen, and one very long, very shapely leg wrapped around his own tree trunks. He smiled, kissing the top of Katarina's head. He'd woken at five a.m. and brought her things into the room so she could shower in his room. Hell, he wanted her to do everything in his room.

Rising, he walked to the shower to rinse off and dress. Despite his years removed from the military, he was still an early riser and couldn't fall back asleep once up. Quickly donning clean clothes, he left the room and walked downstairs toward the kitchen, where he knew the rest of the men would be having coffee already.

As predicted, Zulu, Ace, Ghost, Doc, and Gunner were all seated at the tables talking to George, their resident cook and father figure. George was a seventy-seven-year-old Vietnam veteran who looked and acted twenty years younger. He rode a Harley just like the rest of them, drank, played pool, and had more women than he could handle.

"Well, there he is," grinned Zulu. "Did you dance with the ballerina last night?"

"Fuck you, brother," growled Whiskey. "I don't kiss and tell."

"Ahhh, well, you just gave yourself away, young buck," said George. "Listen to me. She may be younger, but that little girl has been through a lot in her lifetime. If I know nothing else, I know to not let a good woman slip through your fingers. They don't come around twice."

"What the hell would you know, George?" yelled Hawk, entering the room with his twin brother Eagle. "You've never been married."

George turned slowly to look at the men in the room, a fierce expression etched on his face. At his age, his muscles weren't as defined, his shoulders a little slumped, but he could handle any one of these young men in a fistfight. He might not win, but they would limp away in their victory. They all had a healthy respect for George.

"You don't know jack shit about me, little boy," snarled George. "I know this. I know that good women are hard to come by. Pussy? Pussy is easy. It walks in here every Friday and Saturday night, offering it up to any brother who wants it, even this old brother. I had a woman once. The finest woman in the state of Virginia." Hawk swallowed hard, lowering his head in embarrassment.

"I'm sorry, George," said Hawk, genuinely feeling shame for poking fun at the older man. George held up his hand, effectively silencing the younger man and everyone else in the room.

"I'm only telling this story once, so listen the hell up. We were in love. Like to the core, rock your world, nothing else matters, in fucking love. I went to 'Nam, three tours, came back and decided to make a career of it. She waited for me the entire time, waited for my ass to come back to her. Margaret, she decided she would stick with me through it all. We were going to get married 'cept in Virginia they didn't take kindly to a black man marrying a white woman in 1973."

"Fuck," whispered Zulu. He knew the prejudices that still existed for mixed-race couples.

"That's right, young blood, fuck. We decided we would get married in New York instead. Drove all night to get there, got checked into a hotel and everything. Margaret, she got sick the next day, so we postponed it. I'd been worried about her because she'd been losing weight, but she assured me it was just nerves about the wedding. When she couldn't get out of bed on the third day, I knew something was wrong. Took her to the nearest hospital."

The silence filling the room was deafening. The men's faces stared at George, their hearts beating a hundred miles an hour.

"Doc said she had advanced end-stage ovarian cancer. Margaret, Mags, she wanted me to leave her. Said she wasn't fit for me since she couldn't have children." George sniffed, wiping his eyes with the backs of his hands. "Fucking woman, told her I didn't need no kids, and if I did, I'd adopt 'em."

"Jesus, George," said Whiskey. George held up his hand.

"Let me finish. Doc told us she had a few months at best. A few fucking months when I was planning to spend my whole life with Mags. She and I rented a little cabin in upstate New York. I got leave from the military, and surprisingly, they gave it to me. Every day, every fucking day, I would wake up and lean over to make sure she was still breathing. We would have our coffee on the back porch by the lake and just hold hands. I held that woman every moment of every day, knowing the next might be the last."

"Six weeks, forty-three days, and five hours to be exact, she was gone. We went to bed one night, and she leaned over and looked at me and said, 'I'm gonna sleep now, George, but know that I will sleep knowing that I was loved by the most amazing man in the world.' I woke the next day, and she didn't. How fucking fair was that? I buried her, the only one who wept over her grave 'cuz she'd given herself to a black man." He said the words with disgust and hate. Zulu's body shook with anger and emotion.

"I went off to finish fifteen more years in the military. I took every dangerous mission they would give me. I think I was trying to kill myself. I wandered after that, looking for something, anything to hold onto. Then I found you boys. If ever there was a group that needed direction, it was the fucking lot of you." They all laughed, and George looked up, wiping his eyes again. "Listen, this is for you, Whiskey, but all of you... life gives no guarantees. Take what you have now. Take it and hold it, love it, treasure it, treat it with kindness and respect, hold it close, but don't smother it. It's life, son. It's life and love, and if you turn your back for one fucking second, you'll miss it."

"Oh, George," said Grace, standing in the door. She'd come in at the beginning, silently standing in the doorway to listen to the older man. She moved slowly toward her friend and cooking partner, wrapping her arms around his sturdy body. "I love you, George."

"I know you do, girl," he said, kissing the top of her head. "And I know that big ugly asshole behind you loves you and this baby. I can't wait to be the surrogate grandpa for him. Alright, enough of all that. Let me make breakfast."

The men were quiet for a few minutes, and as others started to join, the conversation picked up as they talked about Krevnyv and Omar, the bike shop, and everything else. Whiskey stood to refill his coffee mug and nudged George in the shoulder.

"Love you, old man," he said, growling at the older man.

"Love you too, white boy," he said, smiling back at the younger man.

CHAPTER TEN

Kat was a little disappointed when she woke to find the bed empty but then, seeing that it was almost ten o'clock, she knew she'd slept longer than anticipated. She stretched, feeling the ache in muscles she didn't know she had. As a dancer, her legs and feet were often aching or bleeding for days after a heavy practice or workout. She was aching from a completely different workout that had her smiling.

Showering, she touched her sensitive pussy, reminding her of her night of passion. When she stepped out, she quickly dried her hair, leaving it down her back, and then slid into a pair of black yoga pants and a big green sweatshirt with the Marine logo on it.

Once downstairs, she grabbed a cup of coffee from the kitchen, noticing that George was already prepping for lunch.

"Good morning," she said, smiling at the older man. She'd only met him briefly the night before, but he had kindly eyes and a hidden intelligence that she suspected he tucked away for special occasions.

"Good morning, Sunshine!" he said, smiling at the girl. "Aren't you a picture worth a thousand words this morning?"

"Thank you, George! That's very nice of you considering I still have a black eye and a bruised face," she grimaced, touching the tender cheek.

"Wouldn't matter, Sunshine. You're still beautiful." She kissed his cheek as she grabbed one of the biscuits warming on the top of the stove. "Everyone's in the restaurant. We don't open until two on Sundays." She nodded and waved as she walked down the long hallway. Opening the first steel door, she smiled at the six rooms, three on one side, three on the other, that the single men used to entertain the free services offered by some of the young women who came to the restaurant. Whiskey explained to her the previous night that, unlike many MCs, theirs did not have sweet butts, club whores, or kutte sluts, whatever you wanted to call them. The restaurant was a working, family restaurant and bar, so no nudity was allowed, although many of the young women on Friday and Saturday night tested the limits. If the guys wanted some free pussy, they used one of the six available private rooms. But no one, absolutely no one, stepped through the second steel door unless they lived there.

She stepped through the second door, and sure enough, almost the entire crew was engaged in hanging Christmas decorations again.

"There she is!" yelled Bree, rushing toward the young woman. She kissed her cheek and gave her a slight squeeze. "How are you feeling?"

"Good," she said, blushing slightly. She lowered her voice so only Bree and Grace could hear. "Really, really good, ladies."

"Yes!" yelled Grace. Kat's face turned beet red, and she giggled. "We needed more girl power around here, honey. I'm so glad you're staying."

Kat's eyes met Whiskey's, and he motioned for her to come sit by him at the table, except he didn't give her a chair, he pulled her onto his lap, one big arm draped around her middle. He leaned in, smelling the enticing fragrance coming from her clean hair. Remembering the feel of the silkiness against his body, he instantly went hard. Kat picked up on it as well and wiggled her ass against him.

Ace walked toward them with a stack of papers, glasses shoved on top of his head, and a pen tucked behind his ear.

"They've hired more men," he said casually. Silence greeted him, and he looked up, seeing Kat's frightened face. "Shit. Sorry, Kat."

"Don't be," she said casually. "We all knew he would do this. He's angry, and he's trying to sell his own daughter. I ran. I knew he'd be pissed."

"Yea, well..."

"Well what, Ace?" she asked, staring at the man.

"I, maybe you want to talk about this in private first," he said.

"What the fuck are you talking about, Ace?" growled Whiskey.

"No, no, it's okay, Ace. Anything you have to say, you can say in front of the group. Everyone's involved. It's only fair."

"Okay. A few things. Anton Krevnyv is not your father." Shock filled her face, and she felt herself start to sway. Whiskey's firm grip held her strong, and she stared at the young man again. "I'm sorry, Kat. This is why I said we should talk in private."

"I... I don't understand. Was my mother..." Ace shook his head.

"You are the daughter of Dimitri Krevnyv, Anton's older brother who was killed while serving. Your uncle took you in to raise you as his own."

"That's... that's why he said it was time for me to pay. He's selling me to make me pay for the life he's given me. He's not my father," she said, smiling with relief. "He's not my father. I don't need you to kill him. I can kill him."

"Whoa..."

"Wait now..."

"Hold on a minute..."

The protests came from everyone at the same time. Whiskey finally spoke up.

"Honey, first of all, you won't be able to get close enough with a weapon to kill him. Secondly, I won't let you get close enough with a weapon to kill him. And third, we have to know where the other girls are if they are still alive and if Anton and Omar are the only two involved."

Ace continued as if the other conversations were insignificant. "Omar is staying at a hotel in downtown D.C. He rented out the entire floor. A maid said she went in to clean the room and found a young woman lying on a large cushion, like a dog bed, with a collar around her neck. She was chained to the bed, beaten and bloody. Omar's men came in and told her to leave or die. She reported it to the D.C. police."

"But let me guess. Omar has immunity," said Whiskey. Ace nodded.

"They weren't allowed the warrant to enter the room. They questioned him. He denied everything. End of story. I got a message this morning from Ivan."

"What?!" yelled Ghost. "You didn't fucking lead with that?" Ace looked at him like he was crazy. His calm, rational demeanor took hold.

"No, I didn't lead with that. Ivan is hiding because, as we suspected, Anton now knows that he works for the feds. The women from the ship were turned into the FBI and are being taken care of, but he knows there are at least twenty more being held somewhere. Ivan said he has an inside source. One of Omar's bodyguards is in love with the girl whom we believe was the one beaten and collared. He wants the girl and to get free of Omar. He's willing to help if we can guarantee he and the girl get to freedom."

"What about Anton?" asked Whiskey.

"He's not stopping. It's personal now. She got away, and he doesn't even give a shit about the money anymore. He wants her dead or alive." Kat gasped.

"Brother, we need to work on your delivery," said Zulu, eyeing the smaller man. Ace only shrugged his shoulders.

"FBI wants to talk to her. Ivan is setting a meeting between her and his section chief for tomorrow."

"No," said Whiskey.

"Yes," said Kat.

"Baby girl, we can't trust the feds. We don't know who your... uncle has on payroll."

"If Ivan says it's safe, then I'm going. We can't do this alone. You could send me away. You could put me in a safe house or change my name or whatever, but he would still find me. We have to end my uncle and Omar. I may have information that I'm not even aware will help them."

"She's right, Whiskey," said Ghost. Whiskey stood, Kat now standing as well, hugging herself around her middle.

"Shit, shit, shit, shit, fucking shit!" he yelled. Kat raised an eyebrow and smiled.

"You need to work on your vocabulary, big guy," she said with a grin. "I'm an educated woman who plans on taking the bar soon to keep all your asses out of jail. If you're going to spend a lifetime with me, I need you to use your big words." He looked up at her, shocked at her little speech in front of everyone.

"Lifetime, spend..." he stumbled. She smiled again as his brothers smiled with her. Stepping closer, she put her arms around his waist, looking up at him.

"This is what I mean. Use your big words. Lifetime, Whiskey, Wade." The use of his given name from her lips made him instantly rock hard. "Lifetime, you and me. Married, not married, kids, no kids, I don't care. But a lifetime means we have to do this."

"You want to spend your life with me?" he asked.

"Brother is seriously fucking slow today," said Zulu. Whiskey ignored the big man, only focused on the beautiful woman in front of him.

"Yep," she said, popping the 'p' loudly. "Lifetime. Of course, with your advanced years, you'll have less time than me."

"You did not just call me old," he said, growling at her.

"I think she did," said Doc, grinning at his friend.

"It won't matter, Whiskey. Thirty years, forty years, it won't matter. The only years that will count for me are those spent with you. I love you, Whiskey. I've loved you since I saw you in the library weeks ago."

"I love you too, baby girl. Love you so fucking much," he whispered in her ear.

"About damn time you boys listened to me," said George, setting down three pizzas on the table. "Now eat, celebrate, then make sure this woman is safe, or I'll kick your ass." He winked at Kat and as he passed Gracie and Bree, kissed their cheeks.

"Shit, George's got all the girls falling for him," said Doc.

"Yea, but that right there, man, that's the kind of man I want to be," said Gunner.

"Amen, brother," said Ghost. "Amen."

CHAPTER ELEVEN

Whiskey showed Kat around the property, getting her familiar with all the homes and outer buildings. He took her on a tour of the garage and bike shop, showing her some of the amazing artwork done by Razor, Skull, and Blade. Their painting and artwork on the tanks of the bikes was the major selling point.

Walking back inside Club Steel, Bree and Grace whisked her away to help with the holiday decorations.

"So, what kinds of celebrations do you do for the holiday here? Is Christmas a really big deal with all these big scary bikers?" asked Kat. Bree and Grace looked at her and smiled.

"Honestly? It's all kind of new to both of us. I met Ghost in May when I stumbled, literally, through the gates. I was beaten nearly to death, tortured. I-I was a mess, Kat. I wrecked my car about ten miles from here, and somehow, I think God guided me, but somehow I ended up at the front gates. My ex-husband was psychotic. He killed my parents and our twin daughters on their graduation day and then took me as a hostage and punching bag," said Grace.

"Oh God, Grace, I'm so sorry," she said, reaching for her hand.

"No, no, it's okay. It was the best accident I ever had," she laughed. "Ghost, he's so hard and tough on the outside, but that man… that man carried me so gently for weeks. He hovered over me, feeding me, talking to me when I couldn't even speak for myself. He helped me to heal and then…"

"And then?" asked Kat.

"And then he loved me, Kat. He loved me like no man ever has loved me. He gave me this gift," she said, rubbing her small bump. "I thought I couldn't have any more children, and he gave me this little man. These men are pretty incredible, Kat. They've all served, most in Special Forces. They've been to the worst parts of the world, seen the worst that humanity has to offer, and yet they still fight for the little guy, for the underdog. Do you know that they all left the military, not by their own choice, because they sought justice for twelve little schoolgirls who were kidnapped and killed by terrorists? It was ridiculous. All politics. But not one of them regretted their actions. When they love, they love with all the life and breath within them. They hold tightly to what matters most, and they treasure it."

Kat looked at Grace and took in what the woman was saying. Although she wasn't really old enough to be her mother, she was what Kat would hope for in an older sister. The same could be true for Bree and her wisdom.

"She's right, Kat," said Bree. "God, Doc and I, we had such a rough start. He was so awkward and overbearing and a total alpha asshole. He had an interesting childhood that he just didn't seem to be able to overcome, and I did as well. Together we healed one another. We're still healing one another," Kat giggled, looking over at the big tall man.

"They're all so good-looking," said Kat quietly.

"Oh, honey," said Bree, "that's no secret! Believe me, when you're here on a Friday or Saturday night, you'll notice the young women come in Club Steel that are trying to nab one for themselves. You'll have to show them right away that Whiskey is off the market."

"What about you, Bree? How did you end up here?" she asked.

"Well, at first, it was just me helping Grace to cope with happened to her."

"Not help," said Grace, reaching for her friend's hand. "She saved my life, helped me to find life again with Ghost."

"Love you too, girl," said Bree, smiling. "Anyway, we met initially through Grace. Doc was acting all alpha male badass with me, but damn, he was so handsome and sexy. I knew they did a lot of work with runaways and victims of trafficking and abuse, which is a specialty of mine in therapy. So, on the advice of this girl, I asked him to attend a conference with me in Toronto. He immediately agreed."

"That's so sweet," said Kat, smiling at her. Bree had gorgeous red hair, and without even thinking, Kat reached out to touch it. "Sorry, I just... Your hair is stunning. The color, the texture, it's gorgeous."

"Thank you, sweet girl, but so is yours. Next thing we knew, we were in the middle of a trafficking scenario involving your father, I'm sorry to say."

"Uncle," she said quickly. "He's my uncle, thank God."

"Yes, well, we came back here and found the missing girls. Bad guys put away except for Anton, and now we're in love and engaged."

"Geez, this is really an amazing group of people."

"You're amazing, Kat. A law degree at your age is impressive," said Grace. Kat nodded and blushed, looking down.

"Yes, I said I wanted to take my bar exam soon, and then I want to work with all of you. I sort of skimmed over that a few minutes ago. I need to talk to Ghost about it, I guess."

"Talk to Ghost about what?" said the man from behind her. She jumped, gripping her chest.

"Shit!"

"Sorry, Kat. It's kinda how I got my name. What did you want to talk about?" He kissed his wife and rubbed the little belly, smiling.

"I want to take the bar exam as soon as I'm able. Then, well, then I'd like to work for you, for the Steel Patriots. I could help with all the legal stuff I'm sure you have to deal with, help with warrants, finding homes for the women you rescue, you know..."

"No need to continue," said Ghost, "you're hired." Kat laughed.

"Well, let me pass the bar, and then we can go from there."

"You'll pass, baby girl," came the big voice from behind her. She jumped a little and smiled. Hearing the Christmas music, she smiled. It was the Dance of the Sugar Plum Fairies from the Nutcracker.

"This was my favorite ballet to dance," she said, smiling. Grace perked up, gripping the younger woman's arm.

"Do you have your shoes?" asked Grace.

"Yes," she said, smiling. "They're in my backpack. I carried them with me everywhere. I always looked for a place to dance when the mood struck me." Whiskey ran off behind the steel door, and the women smiled at her.

"I guess we need to restart that song," said Ghost. By the time Whiskey came back, the men were all moving the tables and chairs so Kat would have a clean floor. She laced up the toe shoes, stretching her ankles. Leaving her hair down, she removed the sweatshirt, now in only the black yoga pants and a black camisole. Whiskey hit play on the music, and the sounds filled her soul. This was her happy place. The home her body recognized.

Kat moved across the floor on her toes, her body bending and swaying gracefully with the music. Her long, thin arms stretched above her head, her legs outstretched, then angled artfully above her head. She began her arabesque, moving quickly into a perfect pirouette, spinning again and again.

Whiskey was mesmerized. He'd never seen anything so beautiful in all his life. He was dragged to the ballet by his mother twice and by a date once and swore he would never go again, but if he could watch Katarina dance every time, he would go for the rest of his life.

As the song ended, her long limbs bowed gracefully, and she stood smiling at the silent audience.

"You... you didn't like it?" she asked, fearful. George walked toward her with tears falling down his leathery face.

"Sunshine, that was the most beautiful thing I've ever seen in my life." He hugged her tightly, and the thunderous applause overwhelmed her.

"Jesus, Kat," said Grace, crying, "that was stunning. Absolutely stunning."

"Thank you," she smiled. Each man came up, kissing her forehead or the top of her head. Zulu stepped up and looked down at the tiny ballerina. "Yes, Zulu?"

"How do you spin so fast?" he asked. She looked at the giant, scanning his body up and down. If any one of her former male partners saw this man, they'd run the other way or jump his bones. But in his own way, he was graceful and beautiful.

"Ummm, okay, so are those steel-toed boots?" she asked, pointing to his feet. Zulu nodded. "Okay, just place a hand on my shoulder, keep your back straight." He hesitated, but when Whiskey nodded, he placed his huge paw on her shoulder.

"Now, balancing against me, stand on one foot, don't do anything other than lift one foot. Okay, now lift yourself onto the toe of your boot using me as balance." He looked at the girl like she was crazy but did as she asked. He was surprised that he was able to do it, the steel toe of the boot providing a solid, hard base.

"Okay, I'm going to start backing away slowly. Don't move! Just let your arm outstretch to my body. I won't leave you hanging. Don't get off your toe. Alright, now, I'm going to walk in a circle, just follow with me." Zulu's huge body started to rotate with the help of the tiny woman. It was like a miracle of engineering. "Alright, Zulu. Now, push off. Push off with your other foot, and let your arms propel you in a circle." The men all stared as Zulu looked at Kat.

Doing as she said, he let go of her shoulder and pushed off with his other foot, and rotated on the steel toe, using his arms to spin him. He spun three times before he lost his balance. The huge smile on his face made Kat almost scream with delight.

"That was fucking awesome, Sunshine! Thank you. It was like learning maneuvers in close quarters, spinning and ducking."

"Hmmm, maybe I can make some money training guys on how to be more nimble and quick with ballet moves," she said, smiling. "If I think about it, many of the moves are similar to what I would see in a fight scene at the movies. I mean, if you kept your leg out straight, you could have landed a solid kick to someone's head or upper body." She moved her body side to side. Her leg flew up toward Zulu's head, and he looked at her wide-eyed. Standing completely still, her left leg extended above her head, the toe pointed right at Zulu's face.

"Damn, if you kicked down hard, you could break my nose." She nodded, grinning at the big man.

"Wouldn't be unheard of to train with dance," said Whiskey. "Football players have used ballet for years to improve their footwork. Might be something there. Either way, gotta say, baby girl, that was fucking beautiful, and what you were able to teach Zulu in five minutes incredible." She blushed but kissed him as she reached to take off the toe shoes.

"I hate that he took away my ability to dance professionally, but I love that you and I can enjoy private dances together," she smiled. Whiskey growled, reaching down to throw her over his shoulder.

"Whiskey! What are you doing?" Kat yelped as he tossed her over his hard shoulder, her ass in the air, and her ballet slipper clad feet dangling.

"We're going to have a private dance, baby girl. Just you, me, and those fucking awesome shoes of yours."

CHAPTER TWELVE

Several hours later, exhausted from their private dance, Whiskey was gently rubbing her aching calves, cursing himself for being so selfish as to wish for a private dance. As if reading his thoughts, Kat shoved him to the mattress and straddled his hips.

"I loved doing it, Wade. Dancing for only you was by far the greatest joy of my life," she said, kissing his lips. He gripped her tiny hips and forced her to come forward, so her pussy lay against his semi-hard cock.

"I know, baby girl, but I forgot about your legs. I know they must be hurting."

"They're sore. That's all. They'll be fine, and I will dance for you again – nude," she whispered against his lips.

"Fuck, angel, you're making me hard again," he growled.

"Isn't that what I'm supposed to be doing?" she asked innocently.

"Don't get smart, Sunshine, or I'll spank that beautiful ass of yours." She rubbed herself against him again, and he groaned.

"If you think that will deter me, Wade," she said in a sexy voice against his mouth, "you're wrong. I want your hands all over me. I want you to spank me if you think it will bring us pleasure. I want you to tie me up if you think it will be fun."

"Fuck, baby girl," he said. Gripping her hips, he lifted her and slammed her back down on his cock. "Ride me, baby. Ride me." Kat rocked back and forth, her lithe, lean body bending backward and forward against him. He marveled at her body and took in every movement. She lifted one leg and stretched it out straight, curving over his chest and shoulder. The other she angled back, effectively doing a side split over his huge cock.

Using the muscles in her arms, she lifted herself up and down on him as he gaped at the marvel of her body.

"Fuck, baby girl, fucking hell, that's fucking hot…"

"Big words, baby, not just fuck," she grinned. He slapped her ass cheek, and she yelped, loving the sensations as his cock hardened and enlarged inside her. Shit! He was loving this. "Again." He slapped her ass cheek again, and she moaned, grinding her pussy against him.

"I'm cumming, baby girl. Cum for me…" She nodded, rubbing her clit as he moved faster and faster inside her. Kat reached up with her other hand and squeezed her breast, twisting her own nipple hard. It was like a sudden explosion of pleasure and pain in her body. She shook with a satisfaction unlike anything she'd ever experienced.

Bringing her legs back toward her body, she slid to Whiskey's side, breathing heavily.

"Fucking hell, baby girl, I don't give a shit about big words. That was fucking amazing, Kat. I've never, and I mean never, had that kind of pleasure with a woman. You're fucking amazing, baby, amazing."

"So are you, Whiskey. I meant what I said. I love you. I know I said it in front of all your friends and probably made you uncomfortable and all, but I meant it. I meant every word of it. I've loved you since that day in the library, and I want to spend the rest of my life with you and make you happy and make love and make babies and…"

"Baby girl," he said, grinning down at her, "you're using too many big words, and you're babbling. I love you too, Kat. You didn't embarrass me downstairs. They're my family, my brothers. I love them all, and I love you. Planning a life with you, filling your belly with my babies, honey, that's fucking amazing. It will happen, Kat, but first..."

"First, we have to get to Omar and Anton," she said quietly.

"Yea, baby," he kissed her forehead and slapped her ass cheek. "Let's get up, sexy. I'm sure the others are having dinner downstairs. We should join them." She nodded as they cleaned up and dressed. By the time they got downstairs, George had a private meal for them waiting at the reserved tables. Ace filled a plate and then stopped in front of Kat and Whiskey.

"Hey, Kat, can I see your phone for a bit?" he asked.

"Ummm, sure," she said, handing it over to him. Whiskey stood and followed Ace, as did Ghost.

"What's up, brother? Why did you take her phone?" asked Ghost. Ace squirmed a bit, and Whiskey had the feeling he wasn't going to like what the man was about to say.

"I... I've been blocking the calls and text messages to her phone from Anton." Ghost folded his arms over his chest, and Whiskey looked like he was going to kill him. "I had to. Sooner or later, she was going to pick up on the call, and that would lead them straight to here. I've been routing the calls to the cell phone number for Calvin Edgewood."

"Who the fuck is Calvin Edgewood?" asked Whiskey.

"He's a long-haul trucker currently making his way from Wisconsin to New Mexico." Whiskey couldn't help but laugh.

"So will you be able to hear the messages?" asked Ghost.

Ace looked offended at first but then nodded at the two men and turned to take his meal and the phone back to his quiet space. Ace didn't like noise or crowds. He tolerated the brothers and now Grace, Kat, and Bree, but he didn't do much more than that. He was definitely a weird one.

"Fuckers, scary genius, brother," said Whiskey.

"Yea, man. Let's see what he finds. Tomorrow we ride with you and your woman to the FBI headquarters and see what we can do about stopping this shit." Ghost looked at the concern etched on the face of his friend. "Hey, brother, he has no clue we're connected. None. Our job will be to make sure no one sees her going in or out of the FBI."

"Yea, I know. I trust Ivan. It's just all those other assholes I don't trust." Whiskey returned to the table, joining in on the light conversation, careful not to raise any suspicions with Kat. Thirty minutes later, he and Ghost both had a text from Ace to come immediately. They casually stepped away from the table, signaling to the others to keep the conversation going.

Entering the private space of Ace was something they all had mad respect for. He liked things neat, orderly, and in a very specific way. Don't touch anything, don't bring any food or drink into his space, and damned sure don't touch his computers.

"What's up, brother?" asked Ghost.

"His last text message. You need to read it."

My little whore of a daughter. You will find that your punishment this time will leave you barely breathing. Omar and I have something special planned for you. If you think breaking your legs was bad, you haven't seen anything. Breaking your spine might be better, but then again you won't be able to feel the punishment we have planned. I will find you and I will kill everyone around you.

"Fuck, if she reads this, she'll turn herself over to him," whispered Whiskey. "I know her. She'll think we're all in danger."

"I'm going to tell her I broke her phone trying to remove all the tracking software. I'll give her a burner, so she has a way to communicate with you. I'll put in your phone number, Ghost's, Grace, me, and Zulu. That should be enough to get her help if she needs it." Ghost nodded, staring at Whiskey.

"Brother, we knew he was going to be vicious about this. We will keep her safe."

"Uh, yea, about that. I've been working on something," said Ace, smirking as he ran his hand behind his own neck. "I, well, with Grace and then Bree, I just figured we might need this. It's a bracelet. It can't be removed unless you have a key. In the clasp is a tiny tracker. It's good for up to a hundred and fifty miles. I just figured..."

Whiskey grabbed the smaller man from the chair and kissed his cheek, hugging him tightly. He felt Ace stiffen in his grasp and realized his mistake. Ace did not like to be touched by anyone. No one was quite sure why, but they respected his need for distance.

"Sorry, brother. Sorry, Ace. I'm sorry, brother," he said, pushing the man back. Ace closed his eyes, his breathing heavy. Ghost held onto Whiskey's arm.

"I'll get Doc," he said.

"No," said Ace, "no, I'm fine. Sorry about that. You guys know, I just don't like to be touched. It's okay. I'm sorry, Whiskey."

"No apology needed, brother. That was my fault. This is genius, Ace. I'm sure the girls will be grateful for the added protection." He nodded, handing the men the three bracelets. Ghost looked at the box and saw ten more bracelets inside. Raising an eyebrow, Ace grinned.

"You guys are finding women left and right here. I thought I'd be prepared." The men let out a roar of laughter.

"Fucking awesome, dude," said Whiskey.

"Hey, Whiskey," said Ace, "remember to use your big words."

CHAPTER THIRTEEN

"A tracking device? Are you serious, Ghost?" asked Grace.

"Honey, listen to me. Your phones have trackers, but if someone were to take you, the first they would do is take your phone and destroy it or turn it off. This way, the device is on you, and no one knows what it is, other than a pretty bracelet." Grace looked at the piece of jewelry in Ghost's hand. Bree and Kat were eyeing the same thing in Doc and Whiskey's hands.

"I guess I understand," said Bree. "I mean, if I had it in Toronto, the guys would have found us before you got shot." Doc let a long sigh and secured the bracelet on her wrist.

"Okay, okay, I agree to this because I know it will create less worry for you," said Grace. "Besides, it's not bad looking. Ace did a good job creating this."

"What about you, baby girl?" asked Whiskey. "Will you wear this for me?"

"Sure," she said, smiling. "I mean, it's the first gift you've given me and the first piece of jewelry. That's pretty special for a girl." Whiskey grinned at her and leaned forward, kissing her neck, just below her ear.

"When this is done, baby girl, I'll give you so many gifts it will make your head spin." She shivered at the intensity in his voice as he clasped the bracelet to her wrist. Ghost's phone rang, and he looked wide-eyed at the screen. Holding up his hand, everyone instantly silenced.

"Krevnyv," he growled into the receiver. "We've been looking for you, my friend. We have some things to discuss with you about those girls."

"Oh, my motorcycle friend. I have nothing to say to you. However, I do know that you are soldiers of fortune, shall we say."

"No, we're not."

"Whatever you want to call yourselves is not my concern. I have a job for you," he said casually.

"I don't take jobs from you," said Ghost. "You're a fucking child molesting sex trafficker. I have nothing to offer you."

"But my daughter is missing, Ghost. She is a stubborn girl, my only child left living." Krevnyv tried to input emotion into his words, but Ghost could only roll his eyes. "She's missing, Ghost, and her wedding is next weekend."

"Sounds to me like she doesn't want to get married," said Ghost.

"She's a petulant child," said Anton in a firmer, angrier voice. "She needs to come home, and I need you to find her for me and bring her to me."

"No." He could hear the hard breathing on the other end of the line. He knew that Anton must be desperate if he were asking the Steel Patriots to assist in this.

"I'll pay you one million."

"No."

"Alright, let's try this another way. You find my daughter and return her to me, or I will kill that pretty pregnant wife of yours and the redheaded bitch who found my girls." Whiskey saw the face of Kat turn white as she listened to the call. Doc pulled Bree closer.

"You fucking touch a hair on their heads, I will personally cut you into pieces and leave your body for the vultures. You won't fucking come near us, you sick sadistic pervert. I will not bring your daughter to you. Sounds to me like she was one smart cookie leaving your fucked-up ass."

"You'll regret this, Ghost. I can assure you. You'll regret this." The line went dead, and everyone turned to see the sobbing face of Kat. Her skin was white and clammy, sweat dripping down her neck.

"You have to… you have to let me go… you have to…" she cried.

Whiskey started to move toward her, but George stood up and moved around the table, taking the small girl in his arms. He held her tightly to his chest, letting her cry like a father would do. Watching the painful scene made everyone emotional. Kat finally lifted her head and stared up at George.

"What am I going to do, George?" she asked. It nearly fucking broke Whiskey's heart.

"You're gonna let these boys take care of you is what you're gonna do. That man over there. The one with the permanent scowl who doesn't use his big words?" She laughed, and it was the sweetest fucking sound in the world to Whiskey. "He loves you, honey. Loves you something fierce. This ain't their first rodeo. These boys know a thing or two that your uncle don't. Don't let his words make you do somethin' foolish. You let Whiskey take care of you. You do what Ghost and the boys say, and you'll be free in no time."

"Okay, George. Okay," she said, smiling up at the older man. Kat moved toward the arms of Grace and Bree and held onto the women tightly.

"Fucking hell, George, why don't we just have you solve all our women issues?" said Ghost.

"Cuz it's exhausting, and you boys need to learn to understand women better. That woman is scared for you, Whiskey, not herself. You. The big badass Marine sniper. That's who she's afraid for. Take care of her uncle and the other idiot. We need a quiet Christmas." George left, and the men all just watched him walk away.

"See if we can get a hold of Ivan. I don't think it's safe to go into the city. We need to meet on neutral ground. Somewhere Anton and Omar wouldn't think of." Ace nodded and headed back to his space.

"He's not gonna get to her, Whiskey," said Ghost. "But I do think we need to get on the offensive. We need to find him and Omar and take them out. I don't give a fuck about the repercussions." They all nodded their heads, watching as Grace, Bree, and Kat focused on finishing the tree. The three women were banding together in their fear. Ace walked back toward them.

"Gettysburg. They'll meet you at Gettysburg tomorrow. Anton and Omar won't know anything about the place." Ace turned on his heel and walked away. Trying to give some sort of normalcy to their lives, they returned to the decorations.

The tree finally finished was the talk of the evening as the guys shared their favorite Christmas memories from deployments to childhood. Kat learned that Whiskey's parents were still living in Florida, his older sister and her kids only a few miles from their parents. She learned so much about each of the men and women. She treasured every moment.

Back in their room, Kat prepared for bed, watching as Whiskey watched her.

"Hey, can I ask you something?" she asked.

"You can ask anything, baby girl. I might not be able to answer, but I'll do my best." He pulled her toward him as she sat next to him on the side of the bed.

"Why is Ace haphephobic?"

"Half-a-what?" he asked. Kat giggled.

"Why does he have a fear of being touched?" she said.

"Oh, it's not a fear, baby girl. It's just a dislike." She waited for him to expand, and he just stared at her. "Listen, Sunshine, it's not my story to tell, okay, and I really don't know it all. Ace had a pretty horrific childhood. That's all I can say. He's miles different from when he first came here."

"He wasn't on the original team?" she asked.

"No. The original team was Ghost, Doc, me, Tango, Razor, Gunner, and Zulu. We had other guys join us on and off, Blade, Skull, Alpha. Ice and Axe joined a few months back. Eagle and Hawk are much younger but stellar at their work." She nodded against his chest.

"Tired?" he asked.

"A little, but not enough that I wouldn't take some love from you," she smiled.

"How about I just hold you tonight, baby girl? We got our whole lives for loving nights. I just want you in my arms safe and sound."

"That sounds perfect, Whiskey. I love you. I love you so much," she said, rubbing her cheek against his chest.

"I love you too, Sunshine, so fucking much." Looking down, she was already half-asleep. He kissed her nose and turned off the light. Lying in the dark, he stared out the window at the snow falling once again and smiled. If he could keep her safe, they would have a Christmas to remember.

Let me keep her safe, please.

CHAPTER FOURTEEN

Gettysburg was covered in a light dusting of snow. The wide expanse of the field haunting even on a day filled with sunshine somehow gave off a ghostly gloom today; the gray skies filled with flakes, still falling over the battlefield. The park was closed to visitors, except the special group of black SUVs pulled up at the back of the park alone.

In the SUV with Whiskey and Kat were Ghost, Zulu, Gunner, Hawk, and Eagle. In the other SUV were Ivan and Section Chief Will Thomas. Stepping from their vehicle, Ivan moved closer to the Patriot's SUV and tapped on the window.

"Damn, you're still ugly," said Whiskey, rolling down the window.

"And you're still an asshole," said Ivan. "Hello, Katarina."

"Hello, Ivan. Are you okay?" He chuckled at the tiny woman.

"Yes, thank you. I'm fine. My friends tell me you know that Anton is your uncle, not your father." She nodded. "Good, this will make it easier. I need to tell you a story. Come. The park rangers have arranged a nice fire for us." They followed Ivan to a clearing where a roaring fire was surrounded by several log stools. Ghost directed Hawk and Eagle to make sure the area was clear and then keep an eye on the group. Their sniper rifles slung over their shoulders, the twins walked off to search the woods.

"Katarina, since you know of your real father now, I have to assume that you don't know much else about him." She shook her head. "Your father was the oldest son, Dimitri, the one who would inherit everything from your grandfather. When he went off to join the military, his father was proud. It would prove that his family was not just mafia but supportive of their government. Anton was thrilled as well, but for very different reasons. It would give him the chance to move in on your grandfather, twist his mind against his oldest son, and take everything."

"While your father was home on leave, you were conceived. He loved your mother very much, and she loved him. He had no idea you ever existed, Anton convincing your mother it would only create more stress for Dimitri. When he returned to his unit, Anton, who was now friends with many in the upper echelons of the government, ensured that your father would be placed in a suicide squad."

"A... a suicide squad? My father knew he would die?" she asked quietly.

"Maybe, maybe not. Mother Russia doesn't always tell her people everything. Point is, Anton did it intentionally. Your mother had a nervous breakdown right after you were born, and then when she received word that your father was killed, she suffered another and died as a result. Anton... Anton abused your mother the entire time his brother was serving."

"Oh God, I think I'm going to be sick," she said, holding her stomach.

"Baby girl, we can leave."

"No, no, we can't. I need to hear this," she said in a shaky voice, gripping Whiskey's hand. She sat back down, noticing that Gunner and Zulu moved closer to her, giving her the comfort and courage she needed.

"I'm sorry, Katarina. Anton took you and decided to raise you as his own. No one questioned it. No one ever questioned him. It's clear he had a plan for you from the beginning. I'm guessing he knew you'd grow into a beautiful woman since your mother was so beautiful as well."

"She... she was?" Ivan nodded, smiling at the younger woman.

"She was a prima ballerina with the Russian ballet. You look just like her. She had long blonde hair and blue eyes, a true beauty." Kat smiled at the man.

"Why didn't you tell me sooner? We were working together against Anton. You were in that house with me so many times when he... he... why?"

"I should have, Kat. You're right about that, but I worried that if you showed any signs of knowing anything, Anton would move too fast for me to protect you. He connected with Omar about five years ago. They discovered they had a taste for, well, you already know. Difference is Omar doesn't have sex with them. He only abuses them."

"I don't understand. Why was it so important that I be a virgin then?"

"I don't think you want to know that, Kat," he said, looking at Whiskey. Whiskey could feel the anger bubbling up in his body. He knew what sort of deviant ideas Omar possessed.

"I... he... he was going to take my virginity through... through other means," she said quietly. Ivan said nothing, just staring at her.

"Omar cannot have a woman in the biblical sense of the word because his father made him a eunuch. He was a fiercely jealous man and forced all but one of his sons to become eunuchs fearing they would have sex with one of his many wives or girlfriends. What the sick fuck didn't realize was by doing that, he was creating monsters of his sons. The two older sons are known for abusing and killing wives like most of us toss out old magazines."

"My contact on the inside is a guard of Omar's, one of his favorites. Arif is a former Saudi Special Forces soldier. He's big, strong, and a helluva fighter, and he's also a favorite of Omar's, both as a bodyguard and watching him have sex with the women. The current pet of Omar is a young Canadian girl by the name of Juliette. She's only eighteen, but she was seventeen when her father sold her to Omar for a measly two thousand dollars American."

"Jesus," whispered Ghost.

"Arif is madly in love with her and has tried as best he can to protect her from Omar, but it's getting harder and harder to do so. He's at least twenty years her senior, but he seems genuine in his intentions to get her free, even if he has to buy her. Omar likes for him to have sex with the girl in front of him. Arif thinks that, even though he can't have sex with women, he may be gay. He likes for Arif to be seen, but not the girl. Arif continues to do as he's asked because at least he can control that part of it for the girl. The problem is Omar beats her when he's not around. Two nights ago, he returned to find her nearly bleeding to death on the floor."

"Oh my God," said Kat. "Is she alright? Is she alive?"

"He carried her out of the hotel, and they're in a safe house for the FBI. Arif has given us everything we'll need to make sure Omar is taken from the country. However, we don't want him to leave. We want him dead. That's where you guys come in."

"Come again?" said Ghost. "Are you saying you want my men to take out a foreign national who has diplomatic immunity?"

"Yes," said Section Chief Thomas. It was the first thing he'd said since sitting down. "Yes. We can't do it. It would be traced to us since we are the only people who have knowledge of every event, every meeting, everything he attends. We want this to look like a robbery or carjacking gone wrong. Omar is scheduled to visit a children's hospital of all the things tomorrow afternoon. We have the route, the details, everything. We need your men to stop the vehicle, kill Omar and his men."

"And how do I know you won't come knocking on my door with an arrest warrant when this is all over. When you get what you want?" asked Ghost.

"You have my word, Mr. Stanton." Zulu let out a loud huff of disbelief, his big arms folded across his chest.

"It's Ghost, and forgive me, Section Chief Thomas, but I don't give a flying fuck about your word. I've worked for the government. I know very well how they screw you over and take back their word."

"He won't," said Ivan, holding up his phone. "I have everything that was just said recorded, and you have my word that I will send you a copy of the recording."

"Funny," said Gunner, "so do I. I mean, just in case yours gets lost or something." Ivan grinned at the man.

"If Omar is out, Anton will panic. It could make him more dangerous, but we'll have to be prepared for that. He'll have no immediate buyers for the girls, and he'll have no source of money for you.

Your uncle is flat broke, and he's already battling the other families for total control."

"How is that even possible, and what does that have to do with me?" she asked. Ivan laughed and shook his head, looking at her. She had no clue.

"Jesus, you really don't know," he gasped. Kat shook her head again, staring at the men around the fire. "The money, the houses, cars, islands, mansions, fuck you have a castle in Ireland. They're yours! They belonged to your grandfather and then your father, but Anton took control since he wasn't going to tell you about your paternity. Once you turned twenty-three, everything legally was to go to you. That's why he was trying to get you married to Omar. Under Saudi law, you can't own property. Omar would sign it all over to Anton. That was their agreement. Omar would get a small island off the Amalfi coast to keep the girls stashed."

"Holy shit," she uttered under her breath. "I... I had no idea. I knew he was having financial issues. I never thought... I never put two and two together."

"No way for you to do that, babe," said Whiskey. "That's a shit ton of money, though." She nodded.

"Yea, yea, we could do so much good with that," she said, staring from Whiskey to Ghost. "Think about it. We could build more safe houses for women, and we could have a defense fund for battered women and..."

"Kat," said Ghost, holding up his hand, "honey, that's fucking incredibly generous, but it's your money, hun. We can't take that."

"Yes, you can!" she said, standing defiantly. "If I'm working for you, I can help to support the business too. I want to do this, Ghost. Whiskey? You'll support me, won't you?"

"I'll do anything you want, baby girl, but Ghost is right. That's a fuck-ton of money. Are you sure you don't want to just go off and do something for you?" Her hands were on her hips, and her mouth tightened into a thin white line. Zulu watched her expression and raised an eyebrow, knowing that she was about to blow a gasket aimed directly at his brother.

"May I speak to you for a moment, alone?" she asked. He stood and looked at the other men, all smirking at him. They took a few steps to the side of the circle.

"What's up, baby girl?" She shoved her hands against his chest, and he stumbled a step backwards. "What the fuck, Kat?"

"What part of 'I love you and want to spend the rest of my life with you' did you not get? I don't want to go off and do something for myself with the fucking money my family probably stole or got through unsavory ways. I want to use it to help people. The same people I wanted to help yesterday. Now, if you're having second thoughts about us, Whiskey, just fucking say so. But I will help Ghost and the Patriots whether you decide you want me or not."

She started to walk back to the circle, and Whiskey grabbed her wrist, pulling her close against his body, hugging her possessively, kissing the side of her face as he smiled at her anger. Kat tried to wiggle free, but he was having none of it.

"I'm sorry, baby girl. Listen to me. I'm sorry. I just, Kat, you're so fucking beautiful and young. And now you're rich and beautiful and fucking young. I just, I didn't want to stand in your way, honey."

"I was rich before all this, Whiskey. I had an inheritance from my grandfather and money of my own. Money means nothing, Whiskey. Nothing. I've been alone in a crowded room for years. I've never been more loved or treasured than I have the last few days with you and your teammates. I want to do this, Whiskey. With. You." He kissed her nose and smiled.

"Got it, baby girl, loud and clear." Turning back to the grinning circle around the fire. Ivan continued telling them what he knew of Omar and Anton.

"Omar will be a non-issue as of tomorrow. Anton is what we have to worry about now," said Ghost. "I don't mind helping you take this bastard down, but he's got far-reaching tentacles with the Russian mafia and other families."

"We've spoken to a few of his counterparts in Russia," said SC Thomas. "They're not opposed to Anton having a little accident. Many felt he was getting sloppy in his dealings here, and they were still stinging from him taking over their businesses there. I don't think we'll have any flashback on that at all. Plus, you forget that he's been trying to control the other families as well. Irish, Chinese, Italians, all of them." Ghost nodded, still unsure.

"Kat?" asked Ivan. "Any idea where Anton is hiding now that the house in Georgetown is off-limits?"

"He has several properties, but Anton is a diva all the way. He wants big and ostentatious. My guess is he's either at the estate in the Hamptons or on Chesapeake Bay. My gut tells me he's close."

"I would agree with you," said Ivan. "Alright, let me see if we can get eyes on Anton, and we'll go from there. Ghost? If I give you the location of Arif and Juliette, can you help them?"

"We can get them to the club and settled there. They'll probably be better protected and safer, but once Omar is taken out, it won't matter. They'll be free to move on."

"Let's wait until Omar is gone for good tomorrow. Once that's done, he'll be in less danger." They nodded, walking back towards the SUVs. Ivan never even heard the twins, but as they approached the vehicles, he noticed that both were behind him. He grinned at Whiskey, sticking out his hand.

"Whiskey, always a pleasure, man." Ivan sounded more British than Russian, but he grinned at the big man, shaking his hand.

"You know, you're only the second Russian I've liked," he said, grinning at Ivan.

"I'm not Russian," she said, elbowing him. "I'm an American." Ivan could only laugh.

"Good luck with that one, brother." The car was silent on the way back to the club. The men were careful not to discuss anything in front of Kat that might leave her vulnerable. Kat was deep in thought when they finally pulled in. Ghost turned in his seat to stare back at her.

"I know I don't have to say this, Kat, but I will. Nothing that was talked about today gets repeated. Nothing. Not to Grace. Not to Bree. No one. Understood?" She nodded, suddenly fearful of the big man in the front seat.

"I'll go see if George needs help with dinner," she said, opening the door. She kissed Whiskey and disappeared into the restaurant.

"Eagle? Hawk? Feel like doing a bit of hunting tomorrow." Both men smiled and nodded. "Gear up, full fucking gear up. I want both of you back, no scratches. You can probably bet he'll have bullet-proof panels and windows. Take whatever you need. Use the armor-piercing."

They leapt from the vehicle and ran toward the back gates of the club leading to the private residences.

"You just unleashed those two idiots in the candy store," said Gunner. "Made their fucking day."

"Yea, well, let's see if we can get one asshole dead and then deal with the other."

CHAPTER FIFTEEN

Omar stared at his new pet from his perch on the huge king-sized bed. His rotund belly was hidden beneath his robes. His long legs stretched out before him as he watched her. Her pert tight little white bottom was bare, her full breasts swinging with every movement.

He was still perturbed that his guard, Arif, had run off with the other pet. He didn't really care about the girl. Girls were a dime a dozen literally in his world, and he hadn't paid all that much for that one. He was more disturbed that his guard left him, his most trusted, beautiful guard. He groaned as his pet crawled around the room as he directed her to do, making lazy circles on the carpet.

His other guards were not as pretty as Arif. They were all tall, hulking men, but Arif had been tall, muscled, and beautiful. He'd watched him fucking his little pet and wished it was him. Yes, just like that, he thought he'd wished it were him bent over in front of Arif. Yes.

His guards watched the young girl crawling around the suite. They gave no indication that it turned them on or excited them in any way, only watching the young girl, hands folded in front of their crotches. He knew for a fact Imed enjoyed playtime with Omar on occasion. The bodyguard had a desire for boys but was satisfied with other men as well. They'd had several moments of enjoyment, so perhaps he had no interest in the girl. Jamal appeared to be hiding something, though.

The new pet was a blonde instead of a brunette. She wasn't as beautiful as Katarina, but she was still lovely with big green eyes and wavy golden hair. Such a treat since all the women in his country looked the same.

"Jamal?" he called to the guard on the other side of the room.

"Sir?" he said, quickly moving to stand in front of Omar.

"Are you married?" he asked, eyeing the big man up and down. Jamal squirmed at first, not daring to look down into the eyes of the man he loathed, the man who was holding his parents' safety over his head for his service.

"No, sir."

"Do you like my pet?" he asked.

"She's lovely, sir." Jamal tried to show no emotion, but it was difficult. The girl was beautiful, and he'd caught her looking at him more than once with pleading eyes, but also something else, something he didn't dare explore on a child.

"Would you like to taste her?" he asked.

"Sir?"

"I asked if you would like to taste her, Jamal. It's a simple enough question. I'm offering my little pet up to you." The man's eyes widened, wondering if it were a trick of some sort. Omar didn't even wait for his response. "Pet? Come here."

She crawled to the man, her knees raw and burning from the carpet. Her face covered in dry tears.

"Sweet pet, why are you crying? I'm not going to hurt you. I want you and Jamal to have some fun. Take his cock out and suck it." Her eyes grew big, and she kneeled back against her heels, looking up at the big man. He looked as though he didn't want this any more than she did. "Don't make me tell you again, pet. Take out his cock and suck it, and you better make him hard."

She nodded and looked back up at Jamal. He'd been kind to her, giving her ointment for her knees those first few days. Now, kneeling before him, she unzipped his pants. The outline of his semi-hard cock could be seen beneath his trousers. As he slid his pants down, she pulled him from his boxers and gasped. He was enormous. His cock was as thick as her forearm and almost as long. He would tear her apart.

"Oh, my goodness," smiled Omar, "you've been hiding your assets, Jamal. Get to work, pet." She wrapped her lips around his head and began moving up and down, her tongue wrapping around him. His eyes darkened, looking down at the petite blonde. He knew he was too big for her tiny mouth and most definitely for her little pussy. He also knew the sick fuck he worked for wouldn't let it go.

"I need to sit, sir," said Jamal. He nodded at the man as they moved away from the bed where his lazy, fat ass was perched toward the sofa. It was far enough away that Jamal could whisper to the girl and warn her of what was to come. He hated this. Hated that his body was reacting to the young girl, hated that he had to play into his sick fucking games, hated that this poor little thing would be destroyed by his own body.

From this vantage, Omar could see his pet's backside and her bobbing head. Thanks to Jamal's jumbo cock, he could even see it from the bed.

Tears were streaming down the girl's face as she tried to take more and more of him. He held her head, his breathing becoming rapid. She was really good at this, and lord knew he needed to fucking blow, but he didn't want to hurt her. She was a child caught in this sick fuck's game.

"Fuck her," said Omar. Oh shit. He was going to rip this little girl in two. No woman had ever been able to accommodate him fully, and this was no woman. She was probably only sixteen or seventeen years old. Jamal nodded. He pulled the girl towards him and had her straddle him.

"Are you a virgin?" he whispered. She nodded, tears streaming down her face.

"Sir, may I have some lube? It might be better for pet if this is her first experience."

"No."

Jamal ground his teeth together.

"Listen to me," he whispered against her lips. "I'm going to try and get you wet and ready for me, and then, I'm sorry, it's going to hurt." She nodded and then kissed him. He opened his eyes, shocked at the feeling of her lips against his. He was twenty-nine years old, and she was a child. This was wrong in every way.

"It's okay," she said against his mouth. "I know you're trying. It's okay." Poor kid probably had a shit life before this. He knew she'd been purchased from a dealer taking payment for her whoring, drug-addicted mother.

Jamal ran his finger between her sweet lips, sliding one inside her tight hole. Have mercy on his miserable soul. She was like a vise against finger. He slid in two, and she let out a moan.

"No enjoyment, pet. Spank her, Jamal." Jamal slapped her ass cheek with a loud crack. She jumped but held in her squeal. He looked into her pretty blue eyes and saw fear but something else. Shit, she was hot for him. She had lust in her eyes. Fuck!

He slid in three fingers, and she bit down on her lip to not let out a sigh or moan of pain. He was stretching her, and she was really in need of stretching.

"Enough foreplay. Fuck her," ordered Omar. Jamal thought to ask for more time but knew it would only anger the man.

"I'm sorry, sweet girl," he whispered. She nodded as he positioned his cock at her opening. Gripping her hips, he thrust up hard, breaking through her barrier and so much more. He was certain that it must have felt as though she were giving birth, given the size of his cock and its girth. He felt the blood coating his cock and looked down to see there was more than should be for a virgin. He'd torn her open. He knew he would. He was too big for her and hadn't been able to prep her enough. Her mouth was open in agony and pain, but she didn't let a sound escape. Tears flowing down her cheeks, she stared into his dark eyes and could only nod.

"Blood!" said Omar excitedly. "Lovely, you've torn open my pet. Well done, you big stud. Now fuck her, move. I want to see your cum dripping out of her!" Jamal couldn't help his body's reaction to the young girl, her tight virginal pussy squeezing him. He started to move slowly at first, but then she moved with him. She rocked her hips against him, and it was the sexiest thing he'd ever seen. She was just a girl, a fucking teenager, but she'd taken all that he had ripping her tiny body open, and now she was showing him she understood.

"That's it, sweet girl," he whispered as he kissed her, "take it. Enjoy it with me. You're beautiful, sweet pet, beautiful. Don't let him destroy you." Omar watched as the man pounded his monster cock inside the tiny girl. Blood dripped from her ass cheeks, and his whole body shook with excitement.

She leaned forward and kissed him tenderly, her tiny hands behind his neck.

"Cara," she whispered, "my name is Cara, and I think I love you." He could only smile at the innocence of the girl.

"I'm going to cum, sweet Cara. Come with me. Show me that you got some enjoyment from this," he said. She nodded again, and he felt her body shudder with the first racking orgasm of her young life. His own spilled violently within her. He leaned forward again, kissing her sweetly. He carefully lifted her from his still semi-hard cock, blood dripping down her legs.

"Get cleaned up, pet. Jamal, take her into the bathroom and bathe with her. You both need to be cleaned up." He nodded at Omar as he removed his own trousers, lying them on the sofa, now stained with the blood of the young girl. She walked sheepishly toward the bathroom, her head lowered in shame as she walked by Omar. As Jamal passed, he stopped the man.

Jamal gritted his teeth, the hand of the man on his thigh, slowly rising to touch his cock.

"So much blood," he said with wide eyes. He licked his finger and ran it down the side of Jamal's cock. "So much…" Jamal stepped aside and went into the bathroom, not daring to look back at the bastard who held his life in his hands.

"We're going to the children's hospital, Jamal. We'll back in a few hours. Have this mess cleaned up!"

"Yes, sir." He yelled back toward the door. The girl sat on the toilet, not wanting to drip blood on the floor, her face in her hands, soft sobs coming from her little body. "Let me see, sweet girl."

"Cara, it's Cara."

"Yes, sweet Cara. I know. Now, open up for me. Don't be shy. Let me see." She spread her legs, and he winced. It was as he'd suspected. He'd not only taken her virginity, but he'd torn her tiny body. "Let's get you in the bath, sweet one. I'll take care of you. You're going to be very sore for a while. He won't let me take you to a hospital, but I'll make sure you heal." He lifted her to his body, and she wrapped her tiny arms around his neck, hugging him to her. He settled them in the tub and gently washed the blood away, holding her close.

Her sweet mouth begged him to touch her lips again, but he controlled himself, not wanting to damage this child anymore. The shame filling his body was consuming him. He'd never done anything so loathsome in all his life.

"Kiss me," she said with a tear in her eyes.

"Sweet Cara, I wish I could, but you're a child, little one. I'm a grown man. Had I not been forced to do that, I would have not taken your body in that way. I would not have taken that choice from you."

"I… I'm glad it was you. I'm happy it was you. It hurt, but I'll be okay. It will be better next time." He looked down into her blue eyes, and a sharp pain hit his chest.

"Sweet girl, there can't be a next time. You're a baby. I'm a grown man who was forced…"

"You weren't forced, Jamal. You could have said no. You wanted this too. I know you did. And I'm not a baby. I'm nineteen. I just look young for my age." She said, leaning her head against his chest once more.

"Nineteen?" he said. She nodded. She's nineteen. I didn't rape a child. Oh God in heaven, thank you. I didn't rape a child. She's an adult. She's...

"Omar was told I was sixteen by my mother. She thought she could get more money for me if I were younger. I promise you, Jamal, I'm nineteen." He stood swiftly from the tub, water sloshing onto the floor. The pink tinge to the water let him know that her blood was washing away.

"Stand, beautiful," he said, holding out his hand. "We have to go. Now."

"Wh-what? Where are we going?" she asked.

"Away from here. Anywhere far away. You and I, sweet Cara. Will you go with me? I have money, and I'm an American citizen. We can stay in the country. Will you go with me, Cara?"

"With you," she whispered. "You're keeping me?"

"Not in that way, Cara. You will not be my prisoner, but yes, I'm keeping you. You're mine. My girl. Will you be my girl, Cara? I'm ten years older than you, but your sweet body was made for me, Cara. No woman has ever been able to take me as you did. Will you be mine?"

"Y-yes, yes," she whispered. He found clothing for Cara and opened the safe to retrieve his gun and fifty thousand dollars in cash. They would be hundreds of miles away before Omar knew they were gone. He took her youth, but he would give her a life. He wasn't an evil man like Omar. He wasn't a sick pervert. He was simply a man trying to make money for his family back home. Omar would surely take revenge on them, but he would get a message to his parents and tell them to hide. He wouldn't do the bidding of this maniac any longer.

Arif got away. He could too. Omar would be livid. Two bodyguards lost. Two pets lost. Maybe he'd learn a lesson. Don't let your bodyguards fuck your pets. They get attached. He grabbed Cara's hand and pulled her toward the door, looking both ways down the hallway.

"Let's go, sweet girl. Our new life awaits."

CHAPTER SIXTEEN

Hawk and Eagle watched as Omar walked with an air of superiority and self-importance, returning to the vehicle parked outside the hospital where his driver patiently waited. He'd washed his hands at least a dozen times, worried that he might somehow catch a disease from the children. It was ridiculous since most were suffering from cancer.

His route back was a favorite of his, avoiding the majority of the incessant traffic in D.C., instead following along the parkway, trees lining both sides of the road.

The Steel Patriots had men at several spots along the roadway, blocking commuter traffic and clearing the road for their plan to succeed. Once they allowed the SUV to move through, the Jeep following, they would have the road to themselves.

Seeing Omar's vehicle take off, Eagle's identical twin, Hawk, nodded at him as they made their way back to the Jeep. Keeping several cars behind the big SUV, they followed a safe distance until they entered the parkway. Behind them, they saw Gunner and Zulu blocking the road, dressed as public works employees. On the other end, the road was being blocked as well.

In the middle, stood George with a barrier and stop sign to halt the traffic. He allowed several cars to pass and then stopped the SUV with the Jeep now directly behind it.

Hawk stood in the passenger's seat, his upper body exposed through the opening of the top of the Jeep. Lifting the rocket launcher, he pointed it at the SUV. He fired, releasing the missile. The SUV flew into the air, flipping on its side. Glass cracked, and the sound of metal crunching and grating against the pavement filled the air. Once the vehicle settled, no longer spinning, Hawk smiled.

From the passenger door, one man crawled out, lifting his weapon and firing toward Hawk. George dropped the stop sign and fired his pistol, taking the man out easily, leaving only the driver and Omar.

Eagle stepped from the Jeep and moved cautiously around the vehicle toward the windshield. The driver looked at him and smirked, believing the bullet-proof glass would save him. Eagle saw Omar's face filled with fear and smiled. Pulling the weapon from behind him, he pointed it at the driver and fired two bullets that easily penetrated the glass and shattered the man's chest.

Kicking in the remaining glass, Eagle knelt down, grinning at the Saudi. The fear and concern etched on his face made Eagle smile. The sick prick might think he was a God with his men and little girls, but faced with real danger from a real man, he backed down as they predicted he would.

"Howdy, looks like you're in a pickle," he grinned.

"I'm a diplomat! You can't do this!" he screamed.

"Oh, I can, and I will, you sick fuck. You like abusing young girls, destroying them? You buy and sell them like fruits and vegetables at a farmer's market. Is that because you got no dick, old man?" he said, smiling. Hawk knelt beside his brother.

"Can you hurry this up? I want to get home in time for dinner." Omar stared at the exact replica of the other man and couldn't help but grin. Both were easily six-foot-two and two hundred pounds of rippling muscle. Their dark hair and blue eyes made them exotic to Omar, and he could feel the desire in his belly. He'd love to see them side by side, naked. Compare their beautiful bodies.

"What are you leering at, you filthy prick? You like twins? You like looking at identical objects and deciding what sort of sick twisted shit you wanna do? You gettin' a hard-on for me and my brother? Oh, that's right. You got nothin' to get hard."

"How dare you!" he yelled.

"How dare I? How dare I? Let me tell you something, you fucking rotten bastard. It gives me great pleasure to pull your sick ass out of this vehicle and bury you. But before I do that, die knowing this little nugget. Katarina Krevnyv is in love with my friend and brother. They're happy and in love. They will have a lifetime of babies and holidays and vacations while you eat worms, old man." Omar's face was red with anger as he tried to move away from the devil twins.

"Time to meet your maker," said Hawk. Lifting the rifle at close range, he fired straight between his eyes, blowing out bone and brain matter. Just because he felt like it, he fired three more into his body. "I feel better now."

"Me too," said Eagle. "George? You wanna go for ice cream?"

"You boys are sick. Let's go. We gotta pick up the bodyguard and his girl." George jumped into the Jeep and signaled to the others that the deed was done. Traffic was released, and they headed toward the safe house in Falls Church.

The FBI guard at the gate checked their IDs and waved them through. George knocked on the door, and the inside FBI agent said a few things and then disappeared, bringing Arif and Juliette back out.

Climbing into the back seat of the Jeep, George introduced everyone, placing Juliette between him and Arif.

"Where are we going?" asked Arif.

"Somewhere safe, but don't worry. Omar is dead. You're free," said Hawk.

"Free?" he whispered. Juliette leaned into him, hugging his waist. "We're free. We can go anywhere, Juliette, anywhere." She nodded, tears rolling down her cheeks. George watched the exchange and felt a warmth in his chest. All this love was making him old before his time. He wouldn't have it any other way.

Three days later, at a small motel outside Albuquerque, Jamal read that the Saudi diplomat Omar Khanaman had been killed in a carjacking and robbery. He and his driver and bodyguard, Dimon, were all dead. What about Arif? Where was his friend Arif?

Jamal stared at the cell phone, fearful that it was all a trick of some sort. He wanted to hear his friend's voice, to hear that it was all okay. Finally, he dialed the cell phone of his friend in hopes he would answer.

"Hello?"

"Arif? It's Jamal," he said quietly. He wasn't even sure why he was whispering.

"Jamal! I'm so happy to hear from you. Are you alright?"

"I'm, well, is Juliette alright?"

"She is my friend. She is. I heard Omar was killed and felt relief. Did you have to return to our country?" he asked.

"This is my country, Arif. I'm an American citizen as well as Saudi. I-I took his last girl, Cara, and we're finding our way together. She's young Arif. She's only nineteen, and I'm twenty-nine, but she's mine. He made me do things with her. Things she should not have been forced to do, but she wants to be mine." Arif heard the love in his friend's voice.

"I'm very happy for you, Jamal. Juliette and I are happy as well. We've settled in Phoenix."

"We're in Albuquerque!" he said excitedly. "Perhaps we should move closer? Maybe the girls could support one another? We could start our own business, maybe." Arif nodded on the other end of the phone.

"I think it's wise, my friend. Let's start our new lives together."

CHAPTER SEVENTEEN

"One bad guy down. One more to go," said Ghost as the men walked into the club. "Well done, you guys. George? Nice job with the bodyguard. I know you're a little out of practice, but it's always nice to get out and play."

"Makes me feel young again," he said, stretching. "Although sending me with the billboard brothers is bad for my lungs. Who the fuck wears that much cologne on an op?" Ghost shook his head, and the twins smiled.

"You two have fun?" asked Whiskey.

"So much fun, Dad!" said Eagle, clasping his hands together. "Didn't we have fun, Hawk? So much fun!"

"So much fun, Eagle. So much fun." He stared at his brother, their twin humor something that only they generally understood. The twins were known as the pranksters of the team, but they were damn fine warriors as well.

"You two are assholes," said Ghost, shaking his head at the twins. "Nice work. I understand Omar had a few extra holes, but hey, that's not so bad, right? You get the two lovebirds on their way?"

"Yep. One-way tickets. They were relieved to know Omar was dead but were still scared. Feds gave them new identities and some money to get started, but we convinced them that the documents we created would be better, no G-men knowing where they were. Guy is super smart. He's going to start a cyber-security business. He seems decent. Was worried about the girl's mental health and assured us they were going to get therapy. She seemed all in, so I think they might have a shot."

"Maybe we should stay in touch," said Whiskey. The others looked his way. "Friends close, enemies closer, brother, and all that shit."

"We'll make sure they know how to reach us. Ace is good, but we overwhelm the brother on occasion and need to make sure we pay attention to the stress on him. Having someone on the sidelines might be good." They all nodded as Kat, Grace, and Bree came through the doors.

"Is it done?" asked Kat anxiously.

"It's done, Sunshine," said George. "Omar is dead, and he will never touch another girl again. Your fiancé is no more. Now we need to focus on your uncle." George left the group and headed back to the kitchens, finding his happy place amongst his pots and pans.

"How will we get to my uncle? It won't be easy. He's mastered hiding and taking cover with the other rats and weasels." The men looked at her, the disdain and disgust evident in her voice. "My uncle is not afraid of anything other than a loss of power. He wasn't afraid of his wife – who, by the way, was the meanest bitch on the planet; he wasn't afraid of the Russian government, nothing. The only thing… the only thing he ever feared was losing face with his peers in Russia and the other families, which would result in losing power. He'd always hoped to return and lead the motherland mafia as he leads it here."

"Wait, are you suggesting we contact the Russian mob? Like the real dasvidanya Russian mob?" asked Gunner.

"I'm saying that if they knew what my uncle was trying to do, they might cooperate with us, provide some additional manpower. What you've seen so far is just his immediate staff, bodyguards, that sort of thing. My uncle has a small army at his disposal, and if I were to guess, he's calling them all in right now. I think we should contact all of the mafia families. Russian, Chinese, Irish, all of them."

"Christ, Sunshine, you don't ask for much, do you?" said Ghost. "You do realize if we open those gates, we may owe some favors to people we don't want to owe."

"I will speak to them," she said quietly. "If we do this right, we may not owe anything."

"What the fuck are you talking about, baby girl? There is no fucking way I'm letting you in a room full of mafia heads," said Whiskey.

"Listen to me. I've met the heads of these families before. One thing they all have in common—"

"You mean besides being criminals?" said Hawk.

"Yea, besides being criminals," she smiled. "They honor their families more than anything. They honor truth and protection. Yes, they're criminals and do despicable things, but the only time they kill anyone in their family is if there is betrayal amongst them. They will see this as a betrayal to all the families."

"Honor among thieves. How nice," said Eagle sarcastically.

"It's nothing to joke about," said Kat. "When I was a little girl, the families all met at the estate in the Hamptons. Scalia, Laughlin, Wu, and at that time, the Russian head was the Ivanov family. My uncle was simply the head of the Russian families in the U.S. There was nothing more important to all of them than their own families. It was what they were most concerned about, who was protecting their children and spouses, or girlfriends, or wives and girlfriends. Anyway, I remember because they couldn't believe that my uncle, who, remember I thought was my father at the time, placed his son in a private, guarded school, and I was in a run-of-the-mill public school, albeit in a great neighborhood."

"Did the families question it?" asked Ghost.

"Definitely. Especially the Wu and the Scalia family. I think they knew who I was but didn't say anything. My uncle is brutal, not just to me but to those that work for him as well. I remember my nanny disappearing when I was nine because she bought me a yellow dress, my uncle's least favorite color. When I questioned it, I was severely punished." The mood of the room changed quickly, the chill settling over the men and women. Whiskey looked at the woman he was in love with and waited.

"Dancing was the only thing I ever loved and reading," she smiled. "He decided the best punishment for me was to be locked in the basement in a small cage with nothing – no music, no book, no light. I was down there for almost a week. My brother, or I guess cousin, would come down and torment me, turning the lights on and off and leaving me in the dark for hours at a time. One of Anton's guards, Vasily, took pity on me, and when my uncle wasn't there would let me out so I could stretch and get warm."

"Get warm?" asked Whiskey. "Expand, Sunshine."

"He locked me down there in just my underwear. I was only nine the first time and didn't have the common sense to be embarrassed. Vasily knew what my brother, cousin, was doing and snuck me a t-shirt that I could put on when no one was around. I learned to never ask about anything ever again, but believe me, I listened and watched. I kept my head down, studied, and honestly, I was simply planning my escape."

Kat remembered that horrible fear in the basement, the suffocating feeling when the darkness took over, and her only friend, Vasily, was who kept her sanity.

"The families will be on your side if you explain everything to them... if I explain everything to them. They hate my uncle and know that he is trying to take over all their territories. Right now, he's stealing from them, and they don't even know it." Ghost stood from the table, walking around his brothers. He stopped, kissing his wife on her cheek, and then turned to the group again.

"How do we get in touch with them?" he asked.

"I think I can help with that," said Ivan, walking through the doors and toward the table. "I do believe the pretty lady is right. The families will definitely be on board with this."

"Alright then," said Ghost, "let's make friends with the mafia."

CHAPTER EIGHTEEN

Whiskey watched as Kat brushed out her long blonde hair, waves curving down her back, silky even while wet. Her body was pink from the hot shower, her cheeks flush, and the bruising and busted lip fading with each day. She was simply stunning. Legs so long he could explore them for days, the lean muscles curved, sensual.

"Can I ask you something, baby girl?" he said, staring at her as she dropped the towel, pulling his t-shirt over her head.

"You can ask me anything, Wade."

"When you first got here, you talked about finding those girls in the basement and taking the photos that you brought to us. You said you were scared of basements. Was this why? Anton locking you in the cage in the basement?" She nodded her head, nibbling on the lower lip.

"I know it's silly. He can't hurt me anymore, but I've never been able to go in a basement or cellar since that time. I tend to avoid complete darkness." He nodded, pulling her against his chest, her head resting on his shoulder.

"I noticed you leave the bathroom light on at night."

"If it bothers you, I can stop. I don't feel as scared when you're with me," she said, looking up at him.

"Baby girl, if leaving the light on makes you feel better, then by all means, leave it on. Don't you know I'd do anything for you, baby? Anything. I love you, baby girl, and when all this shit is over, you and I are going to talk about our future."

"You've thought about our future?" she asked in a surprised tone.

"I have a lot. Haven't you? We talked about you completing the bar exam and working with us. I just thought the undertone of that was that you and I would be living together, planning a future together. Isn't that what you want?" He held his breath, hoping that he hadn't misread the signals.

"It is what I want, all of it. I just didn't think it was something you would think about. I mean, you're this sexy, muscle-bound Marine who could pick any girl in the city. I just... I just want to be sure that you're sure, I guess."

"What's bringing this on?" he asked. "Where is my confident, sexy baby girl?"

"I don't know. I guess I just don't want you to regret your decision. I haven't had the best example of good marriages or relationships, and I'm worried. You're sticking your neck out for me and the rest of your body," she smiled. "What if you get hurt because of me and then suddenly realize it's a mistake?"

"Baby girl, look at me," he said, placing his thumb under her chin, tipping her face up. "Look at me, Kat. Baby, you are it for me. I would fight mob bosses, fire-breathing dragons, pits of vipers, and a bunch of ballet hating bikers all at the same time for you. Nothing will change after this, baby girl, nothing except you will be mine and nothing will stop us from sharing a life together."

She nodded, and he felt the tears hitting his chest. Hugging her tightly, he pulled the blanket up around them and stared out the window at the snow steadily falling. It was beautiful, the lights catching every flake as they made their way to earth.

"I'll never love anyone the way I love you, Wade. Never," she whispered.

"That's a good thing, baby girl. I'd hate to have to kill someone because they fell in love with you." He kissed her temple and closed his eyes. "Sleep, baby girl. Tomorrow we meet with the Irish. Let's hope their luck is on our side."

CHAPTER NINETEEN

Ian Laughlin stretched his legs in the backseat of the sleek forest green Jaguar. He casually ran his hands along the permanent crease in his custom-made suit pants and brushed an imaginary piece of lint from his jacket. His red hair was sprinkled with silver, his blue eyes still crystal clear, seeing more than he wanted to some days.

It was almost twenty years since he'd taken over for his father. The Italians thought they owned the world of the mafia, that it was their invention. The truth was that the Irish, Russians, and Chinese had their own versions of family business for centuries. The Irish had been fighting in their own country for hundreds of years and squaring off against the English for nearly as long.

Over a hundred years ago, the Irish gangs began their ascent into America. First New York, then Boston, Chicago, and all of the other major cities. They had their hands in money laundering, protection, drugs, and guns. They didn't touch trafficking, just not something any of them felt they wanted to be a part of.

His driver and bodyguard sat in the front seat, making their way up the curving mountain road. Seated next to him was his younger brother, Colin. Colin had no desire to become the head of the family. He was content acting as his second and leading the armies in the U.S. The car slowed and parked in front of a large barn-shaped building with a huge neon sign on the front declaring *Club Steel*.

"We're here, sir," said the driver. The driver opened the door for Ian and Colin, the cold air hitting their fair skin like icy pieces of glass. Stepping into the warmth of the restaurant, a tall, muscular man walked toward them.

"Mr. Laughlin, thank you for coming. My name is Eric Stanton, but please call me Ghost. This is my teammate and brother, Wade English, better known as Whiskey."

"Hello, lads, it's nice to meet ya both," he said with a heavily accented voice. "I admit I was surprised to get a call. I mean, 'tis not every day a gent from the FBI calls a boyo like me from Eire." Ghost smiled at the man, enjoying his accent. They'd worked with a few boys from Ireland while overseas and always enjoyed their banter and their love of beer and whiskey.

"I suppose it does seem odd, Mr. Laughlin, but as Ivan explained, we think we have a common enemy," said Whiskey.

"Aye, the Russian explained alright. And please, call me Ian. This is my brother, Colin." Ghost shook the hand of Colin Laughlin, staring at his face. He seemed oddly familiar, yet he couldn't place where he might have known him from.

"Let's have a seat," said Ghost. "We've got our cook preparing some food for us, and we can share a drink while we talk." They took the table nearest the Christmas tree and enjoyed a sip of whiskey before beginning.

"So, what is it you need from us to bring down the bloody Russian?" asked Ian.

"We need to take out his army, both here and in Russia." Whiskey waited for his response, his glass of whiskey only halfway to his lips.

"Oh, is that all then? Well, I'll call the fairies and the selkies and see if we can get you some magic dust to blow up yer arses that will allow the wee unicorns to fly you under cover of night. Maybe the banshee can sing her sweet song fer ye as well," he said, grinning.

Whiskey looked at Ghost, trying to control his temper. He wanted to jump down the man's throat. This was the life of his woman he was gambling on here. His asinine comments didn't make him feel good about this whole plan.

"I understand how you feel, Ian. Really, I do, but Anton is out of control. He's trafficking children, young girls, selling them to the worst kinds of predators on the planet. He tried to sell the woman I love to a Saudi national who was the sickest fuck in the world."

"And why does your true love matter to me?" he asked. The steel door opened and shut with a bang. Kat walked toward the table. Her hair pulled tight into a top knot, her body encased in a knee-length black sweater dress. Her black boots shined to perfection.

"Hello, Ian," she said with a smile.

"Katarina! Yer a breath of fresh air, ya are. Don't ye look like a fairy princess?" He stood and pulled her into a fatherly hug. Smiling, she then hugged Colin.

"Colin, you're looking as big as ever," she smiled.

"Aye, well, ye know how we Irish love to fight, lass," he smiled.

"Fuck! That's it. I recognized you when you walked in. Colin the Killer. You're the current MMA champion!" said Ghost.

"Aye, that's me. Professional fighter by day. Me brother's right hand by night." His smile was wide and genuine, filled with pride and love for his brother.

"What are ye doin' here, lass?" asked Ian.

"It's why you're here, Ian. I am his true love," she smiled, kissing Whiskey's cheek. "Anton is out of control. He tried to sell me to that Saudi national for him to torture and kill me. If I die, my inheritance from my father goes to him."

"Yer father?" he said, shocked.

"Yes. Anton is my uncle, not my father."

"I suspected the bastard was pullin' one over on all of us. Ye looked nothin' like him or that witch of a wife he was married to." Kat smiled at him nodding her head.

"He's torturing these girls, Ian, Colin. Girls that are as young as eight or nine. Ghost and his team stopped a shipment about a month ago but also found a tractor-trailer with more than twenty girls. All dead. Anton sold me to Omar for a million dollars, guaranteeing him access to part of my inheritance. His plans for me were anything but matrimonial. I'm lucky that Whiskey found me, and Ghost and the team agreed to help me. But he won't stop, Ian. You know that."

"Aye, lass, we know. I like ye, Katarina. I always have, but I'm a businessman. What do I get fer this deal?" Whiskey sat forward, looking at the big redhead.

"You get Anton's business in Boston, the British Isles, Australia, and South Africa. Everything." Ian raised his eyebrows, and Colin let out a low, slow whistle.

"As part of my inheritance, I own Castle Coughlin. It shouldn't belong to me or any Russian. You help us, and that will be returned to you and your family," said Kat, knowing it would sweeten the deal for Ian.

"Who else is involved?" he asked.

"We're asking for everyone to come together, Ian. The Russian family will get all of Anton's business there. The Italians will take over Philly, Miami, and D.C. The Chinese will get New York, San Francisco, Seattle, and L.A." Kat knew she'd piqued his interest. He wanted all of the Isles, but Boston was a matter of pride. His family had been the original Irish family in the area. When Anton came in, he took everything brutally, and Ian had been trying to get it back since then.

"And the other families? They've agreed to this?" he asked.

"We're speaking with them next. Ivan flew to Russia yesterday to speak with them. The Chinese and Italians will be here this afternoon." Whiskey waited as the two men looked at one another, nodding. "Listen, we realize this is unorthodox. I'm doing this for a lot of reasons, not the least of which is that I'm in love with this woman and want to have a life with her. I can't do that if Anton is still out there trying to kill her. I could take him out, but the rest of the Russian family might still come for us, or they might not. I'd rather have everyone on our side. It's a win-win."

"Aye, it sounds that way," said Colin. "Listen, Kat, we've always hated the way that eedjit treated 'ya. We want to help. Really, we do, but we're talking about thousands of men."

"I know, Colin, Ian. But I think if we kill Anton and take out most of his army, the rest will scatter. His men hate him for the most part. His inner circle is loyal, no doubt, but I think if we split off the most loyal, we have a chance."

"Aye, aye, I believe yer right, lass," said Ian. "If this works, my profits will increase by almost four hundred percent, and I won't have 'te pay yer uncle a percentage any longer."

"It will be more than that," said Kat. Ian's eyebrows raised, and he looked at Colin. "Anton has been lying to you all about how much money he's bringing in within your territories. He's skimming off the top, sending product into your territories, and selling it. The women? He's taking the women from your territories. Three of the girls I found in the basement were from Ireland."

"Fecking arsehole!" screamed Colin. Whiskey winked at Kat, smiling. She'd known how to get to them and make them agree with their plan.

"I know we're asking a lot of you. We're not involved in organized crime, and we don't condone it," said Ghost. "In fact, we tend to stop them."

"Aye, lad, we know," grinned Ian. "Ye don't think I'd come all the way up here without doin' me homework?"

"I guess not," grinned Ghost. "Look, I don't want drugs or women coming through our territory, and if someone hired me to take out a truckload of either, I'd do it, but I won't interfere in your business or your territories. My only hard 'no' is trafficking."

"We'd agree with ye there, lad," said Colin. Colin was probably a few years younger than Ghost but still used the term lad with him. It made Ghost smile a bit. He'd love to have the big Irishman on his side in a fight.

"So, we can count on your support?" asked Kat.

"Aye, lass, you have the Irish in yer corner. I'll notify the lads to be ready. We'll coordinate attacks with the other families. I assume that arsehole Scalia will be here?" Kat smiled and nodded. "Aye, well, I hate the bastard, and he hates me, but not as much as we hate Anton."

"Great!" said Ghost. "Why don't we enjoy the food while it's hot and wait on the others to arrive. We'll make a plan from there."

"I do believe I'll join in this little war," said Ian. "I can't let me brother have all the fun."

CHAPTER TWENTY

Vincent Scalia stared at the two redheaded men seated across from him. He respected the hell out of both but hated them at the same time. He'd known Ian for almost his entire fifty-six years of life on this earth. As children, when there were family meetings, they would play on the grounds of whatever mansion they were staying at. As adults, they'd traded fists on more than one occasion.

Now he was listening to the story the military bikers were telling and staring at a man that was about to become his friend instead of foe.

"Vincent, you know how Anton is," said Kat. "He's ruthless and will not stop until he has control over everything."

"I know, child, but you're asking us to risk a lot. I've already lost my own daughter, and now you're asking me to risk everything else." The older man looked at the sweet face of the little girl who used to play with his own daughter when she was younger. Kidnapped four years ago, she was found beaten, raped, and left for dead in her home. She survived but could not live with what she'd been subjected to, finally taking her own life.

"Vincent, Anton is responsible for your daughter," she said quietly. Ian and Colin both looked at Kat and back at Vincent. They'd all been notified when Isabella had gone missing. All agreed to search for the young woman, and then heard she'd died. It was something that made them all sick.

"What did you just say?" he asked, gritting his teeth, his fists clenched.

"Anton, he... he had Dolf kidnap her," she said quietly.

"You... you didn't call me?" he asked angrily. He was failing miserably at controlling his temper and knew that it should not be directed at Kat. But she knew. She had known.

"I did, Vincent. I did. I left you a voicemail telling you I needed to speak with you as soon as possible, but you didn't return my call. I tried to get word to you, and when Anton found out... I..."

"You what, child?" he asked, suddenly more empathetic.

"I was beaten... beaten and starved for a month. He locked me in the basement, refusing to let me out." Vincent closed his eyes, breathing in and out deeply. He was well aware of Kat's fear of the basement and its darkness. She'd accidentally been stuck in his own basement on a visit and was near catatonic when found.

"I know this is a shock for ye, Vincent, but we all knew what a fecked up mind he is. Surely it comes as no surprise te ye." Ian squeezed the other man's shoulder in support.

"No, no, it doesn't come as any surprise. I'm sorry, Katarina. I'm sorry I didn't call you back sooner. I'm sorry I didn't know what was happening. I would have rescued you myself and taken you into my family. I'm sorry for everything, but the one thing I won't apologize for is wanting to kill that bastard."

"On that, we can agree," said Whiskey. "As we've explained to Ian and Colin, Anton is stealing from all of you. He's running drugs and guns through your territories, stealing your profits. He's stealing girls from your neighborhoods, from your countries, and selling them to child predators. This isn't prostitution, Vincent. It's child trafficking."

Vincent stood from the table and ran a hand through his thick salt and pepper hair. As a child, Kat thought he was so handsome and debonair. He was confident yet kind to the children, always giving them sweets. He had a small paunch now where once he was lean and muscled, but she saw glimpses of the man she liked as a child.

"Jesus, Katarina, you risked so much to tell me about Isabella. When I think of what he might have done to you..."

"Don't think about it," she said sweetly. "He wasn't going to kill me. I was his meal ticket. I didn't know it then, but we know it for sure now. My only hope now is to kill him and destroy his armies. If we do this, you get back Philly, D.C., Miami, and other territories once yours."

Vincent turned back to the table and looked at Colin and Ian.

"You're both agreeable to this?" he asked.

"Aye," said Ian, standing to face his old friend.

"Alright then, there are no finer men I'd fight with. I'm in."

CHAPTER TWENTY-ONE

Ghost watched as Ian, Colin, and Vincent chatted over drinks like they were old college friends. It was the weirdest fucking thing he'd seen since he watched a Taliban leader, an Isis leader, a Rabbi, and a Priest have drinks at their base.

"Do you really think they'll do this?" he asked, looking at Kat, suspicion filling his very veins.

"I do, Ghost. They've known each other for years. When I was a child, years ago, the families respected the territories. They would meet once a year to make sure everyone understood the boundaries and what businesses each had so as not to step on toes. When Anton took over, he just basically murdered his way through them all. No one could prove it, but we all believed he killed Vincent's father and mother, Ian's father, and Wu's father. They hate him. They always have."

"And the surprise about Isabella? When were you going to share that with us?" he asked.

"I wasn't going to share it with anyone," she said quietly. "What happened to her was horrific. You have no idea the damage they did to her body. I saw... I saw pictures of it. Anton made sure I did. He used those pictures to scare me into staying all these years. It was... it was more than any human, male or female, could endure. It was the only thing I knew for sure would get him to agree to all of this."

Ghost nodded his head, looking at Whiskey with a silent communication. Kat knew way more than she was letting on, and if she had more nuggets like that one, they needed to know about it.

"The Russians are probably a sure thing. They want their land and business back, and we already know they have no love lost for Krevnyv. What about the Chinese?" asked Whiskey.

"Chen Wu is the wildcard in all of this. The Chinese tend to stay to themselves. Even when the families met, they would come in, conduct business, and leave. They wouldn't even share a meal with the rest of us. Although Mr. Wu was always kind to me and the other children. It seems to be a soft spot for all of them. Wu's are a very tightly knit family. They take no outsiders into their family, and they are quiet about their business dealings. Wu hates my uncle, no doubt about that, but he also hates me."

"Well, that would have been a good fucking thing to know before we invited him here!" yelled Whiskey. Ian, Colin, and Vincent turned toward him, scowls on their faces. Ian stood and walked toward the three.

"I assume ye just told him of Wu?" he asked.

"Sort of, not all of it," she said, biting her bottom lip and looking down at her feet. Whiskey waited patiently, and when Kat didn't speak up, Ian stepped in.

"Wu demanded Katarina for his son when she was just a young lass, sixteen or seventeen at the time. He was willing to wait until her eighteenth birthday, but he wanted a contract for the marriage." Whiskey's eyes grew wide, fury settling in his chest. "It's rare as a unicorn for the Chinese to want to take one outside their family for their own. Wu saw something in Kat, or his son did. Anton would have nothing of it. Offended the 'feck out of Wu."

"Where is the son now?" asked Ghost.

"Well, that's where we may catch a break," said Colin. "He married a few years back. Has himself four bairns and a lovely wife of his own kind."

"He wasn't really angry with me," said Kat quietly.

"He was, lass," said Ian. "Ye shouldn't lie to yer man. Ye refused outright to have the lad, and ye offended him rightly. I believe the exact words were pasty-faced, sweaty-palmed weakling. Granted, he was fifteen years yer elder, but when he sees this one, me guess is he'll be pissed."

"Fuck!" yelled Whiskey. "You need to go upstairs and not be seen."

"No," she said with her hands on her hips. Vincent smirked, Ian and Colin laughing with him.

"I remember that temper tantrum stance," said Vincent. "I believe the last one I saw was over new ballet slippers."

"Well, this isn't fucking ballet slippers! It's her damned life, and I won't risk it because some spoiled kid didn't get her for a wife. She's my woman. Mine and I won't…"

"Wade!" she yelled. Whiskey turned to see her pink face and stopped. "Don't. Don't say anything offensive about Choi. He was a nice man, never did anything offensive or inappropriate with me. I just wasn't attracted to him in any way. His father just believed that whatever he wanted, he would get. They didn't really want me, not in that way. They wanted me to unite the two families. Wu wanted to make sure that I was in his family so that it would force Anton to give him more of the territory."

"Christ, I never thought of that!" said Vincent. "Of course, that would be why. I wondered why they would suddenly choose a woman outside their own culture. Not that you aren't worth it, sweetheart, but it wasn't their style." She nodded, smiling at the older man.

"I know. Believe me, I know. Anton knew it as well." The doors opened, and an older Chinese gentleman entered with a younger version of himself following. "Mr. Wu, Choi, it's lovely to see you both again. Choi, congratulations on your marriage and family. You must be very proud."

Whiskey watched the woman and marveled at her political savvy with these men. She should be working the room at the White House with that kind of talent. What the fuck was she doing with him?

"Katarina," said Wu, bowing slightly to the woman, "it's lovely to see you again. I'm hoping your father is not here."

"No, he's not, and I think you know he's my uncle, not my father." Wu nodded.

"Hello, Katarina," said Choi, hugging the young woman. Whiskey wanted to tear his arms off for touching his girl, but he held back, watching the man. "I'm glad to see you're well and healthy."

"Thank you. I believe you all know Vincent Scalia, Ian Laughlin, and his brother, Colin, and this is Wade English, but they call him Whiskey, and this is Eric Stanton, Ghost." The men nodded at the others, shaking their hands. Ghost waved his arm to the big table, and they all sat down, waiting for the opening to start the conversation. Finally, it was Wu who spoke up.

"So, how are we going to kill Anton Krevnyv?"

CHAPTER TWENTY-TWO

Well, that certainly started differently than Kat expected it to. She thought for sure Wu would come in demanding things and wanting her hide. Instead, he came in prepared to go to war with her uncle.

"I'm glad you're thinking along those lines, Mr. Wu," said Kat. "But I think you need to hear the whole story."

Kat began by telling them of what she'd seen as a young child, all the way up to the kidnapping of Isabella, her attempted escapes from her uncle, and the recent escape from Omar. She then told him of what her uncle was currently doing and his business dealings with the children. Wu stiffened as she mentioned the trafficking, and she wondered if that were good or bad.

"He's taking children?" asked Choi.

"Yes. As young as eight or nine years old. He's not just selling them but selling them to the most brutal child molesters and traffickers on the planet," said Whiskey. "The girls we found a few weeks back here in Virginia were all scheduled to be sold to Russians via Canada. They were going to be trained as sex slaves. One of them was eight years old."

"We have… encountered some of these issues," said Wu. "One of our ships was stopped in San Francisco for a search. We… employ several of the port authority. Typically, we're running our usual contraband of drugs and guns, which is what was supposed to be on this ship. We heard from one of our inside men that they'd discovered more than thirty children in the hold of the ship. He was curious if we were branching out." Choi took over telling the story.

"I met the men at the ship and saw the condition of the children, boys and girls. I assured them they were not part of our business dealings, and the port officer took them somewhere safe to be returned to their families. We learned through the surveillance cameras that it was Krevnyv's men who brought them on board the ship. We've been searching for him since then."

"Jesus," whispered Ghost. "He's out of control. He believes he has ultimate authority over all of you and can control everything. We have to stop him."

"We agree," said Wu. "I have more than three thousand men arriving in the next two days from China. They will cover the west coast for us. I know that the Ivanov's are mustering their armies at this moment as well."

"I 'ken we have as many as that ready as well," said Ian.

"Same," said Vincent.

"I don't have three thousand," said Ghost, "but I can get at least fifty Special Forces and probably another fifty regular military."

"I'd say that's worth a few Irish lads," said Colin, smiling. "We need to make sure Kat is safe and the rest of our women."

"Aye," said Ian. "I'll have the families taken to our stronghold." Whiskey could only marvel at their terminology as if they were preparing for a battle in the 1800s. Who says stronghold any longer? He was trying to picture a massive stone fort or castle somewhere when in actuality, it was probably a mansion on the water.

"My family is secure," said Wu without giving any other information.

"Mine as well," said Vincent. "Where will Kat be?"

"She'll be safe," said Whiskey.

"Listen, Mr. Wu," said Kat cautiously, "I know that we didn't end well the last time we met, but I never meant to offend you or Choi." The old man held up his hand, stopping the young woman.

"There is no need for an apology. I should not have tried to force the marriage. I knew that Choi was not in love with you. He already had fallen in love with Liu. I was being power-hungry and trying to slow down your uncle if I'm being honest. Everything turned out as it should have." Kat smiled with relief as the old man opened his arms to her.

"Thank you, Mr. Wu," she said into his narrow chest. "I always liked being around you. I still have my collection of dragons at home." He smiled down at the girl and laughed.

"I think they did their job. Dragons are to protect you, and I gave you one each time knowing that your uncle was not doing a very good job of protecting you, quite the opposite. I'm glad you've found your own dragon to protect you now," he said, staring at Whiskey. Whiskey couldn't help but grin and nod.

"Alright," said Ghost, "let's get this settled. We're going to need to plan this operation to the second for it to be successful."

"Aye, that's right, boyo, and you know how to plan an operation, but we operate in a different world," said Colin, smiling. "Watch and learn."

CHAPTER TWENTY-THREE

"So, you're suggesting that we first disrupt his flow of business?" said Whiskey, looking at Wu.

"Yes. If we stop his shipments, he has no money. No money means no payroll. Katarina? You need to claim your inheritance immediately. Contact the estate attorney and get everything settled in your name." He looked up at Whiskey and back at Katarina. "Are you in love with her?"

"Yes, sir, I am," he said confidently.

"Are your intentions to marry her?" asked Vincent. Whiskey raised his eyebrows. It was as if these men were taking on the surrogate role of father with Kat.

"Yes, my intentions are to marry her." Kat smiled, wrapping her arms around his waist.

"Get a priest now," said Colin.

"Wh-what?" Katarina's eyes grew as big as saucers. "N-no, we can't get married right now, not with all of this. We've only..."

"Ye can, and ye will lass," said Ian. "If yer married, he's no right to your fortune. Ye marry this lad, and he'll have the rights if somethin', God forbid, should happen." Whiskey frowned at that knowledge, but it was Ghost that stepped forward.

"He's right, brother. If you two are married, he gets nothing. She needs to claim what's hers, transfer it to an account in both your names, and you need to marry immediately." Katarina's face was pale, her knees suddenly wobbling beneath her.

"Kat," said Whiskey, pulling her to the side, "we don't have to do this, honey. I don't want your money. You know that. We can find another way. We'll..." She held up her hand, her fingers lightly touching his lips.

"Do you love me, Wade?" He nodded, smiling at her. "Do you want to marry me?" He nodded again. "Then this is the best way, all the way around. It's backwards as all get out, but I can get the money, homes, everything transferred to an account that's ours, and then we marry."

"Are you sure, Kat?" She kissed his lips sweetly and nodded.

"Never more sure of anything in my life. He'll know, Wade, Ghost. He'll know that you're involved now."

"Was gonna happen sooner or later anyway, Sunshine," grinned Ghost. "Let's get this started. Ace can get the account set up for the two of you and help with the transfer. Kat? Go sit with Ace to get this done. Whiskey? See if George still has his preacher's license."

"She needs a priest," said Vincent. "In the eyes of the Russian church, they won't consider her married. If we can get a priest in, it will be more secure for her." Whiskey nodded and headed back to George, who seemed connected to every clergyman in a hundred-mile radius.

Ghost sent out a text to all the brothers to meet in the main room immediately. Within an hour, the women were preparing for a wedding. George was cooking a feast, and the men were preparing for war.

In Ace's den of solitude, Kat quietly took a seat next to him but with a respectable distance between them. She watched Ace peck away on his computer, setting up the joint account for her and Wade. She didn't question him, didn't ask him anything, just watched. Fifteen minutes later, he turned to look at her.

"Thank you for giving me the quiet I needed," he said. She nodded, smiling at him. "Now, your account information?" She slid a sheet of paper across to him, and his brows went up.

"This is all yours. Now yours and Whiskey's?" She nodded again. "Ummmm, wow, I don't think I've ever seen so many zeroes as it relates to a bank account."

"I want this account placed into a 501C for the Patriots to use."

"All of it?" he squeaked. She smiled, nodding silently. "Kat, that's over fifteen million dollars."

"I know how much it is, Ace. I saw the numbers the other day when we found out from Ivan about all the accounts. There's more than enough there for Wade and me to live on for the rest of our lives. I want to make a difference, and this money will help the Patriots to help these women and children. The rest, well, the rest I'll give to various charities. The only thing I want to keep is the house on the Chesapeake. It's beautiful and could be used as a good retreat for all of us."

"You're sure?" he asked again.

"I'm sure, Ace." He nodded and went to work, his fingers flying over the keyboard. Within an hour, all the funds were transferred to the account, now in the name of Wade and Katarina English, with fifteen million in a non-profit account named justly Isabella's House. Vincent would love it.

"Okay. All done."

"Thank you, Ace. I'd... I'd hug you, but I know, I mean, I don't know. I mean..."

"It's okay, Kat," he said, giving the woman a rare smile. "Listen, I don't share what happened to me because it doesn't matter anymore. I just don't like to be touched. That's all." She nodded.

"But Ace, what if you found a woman you fell in love with? What then?" He stared at her for a long moment.

"Well then, I guess I'll deal with that when the time comes, beautiful." She stood and then turned back to him.

"Can I at least shake your hand?" she asked pleadingly. Ace nodded, tentatively extending his hand in her direction. Her delicate fingers slid into his palm, and he swallowed, watching his big hand envelope hers. She gently shook one time, dropped his hand, and, turning, left the room.

Ace stood for several moments waiting for the panic to set in, for the feeling of compression on his chest to suffocate him, but it never came. The ballerina unwittingly had given him a gift beyond anything money could buy. She'd given him the gift of non-threatening human touch.

CHAPTER TWENTY-FOUR

"This can't be right," said Whiskey, "this much money does not exist." Kat laughed at him and nodded her head.

"It does, and it's ours, although I plan on giving most of it to charities. The castle will go back to Ian and his family, as it should. Their family owned that property for centuries before my uncle stole it from them. The lands outside of San Francisco will go back to Mr. Wu and his family, and the stud farm in Pennsylvania will return to the ownership of the Scalia family. All of the properties in Russia have been returned to the Ivanov family as a sign of good faith. We can only hope that they see it as such and will follow through with helping us."

"I can't fucking believe you did all this, but I can tell you one thing, honey. Giving all this to charity? I fucking agree with that, baby girl," he said, kissing her forehead. She was dressed in a simple wool skirt and white silk blouse. Her long legs held up by a pair of cream-colored pumps. Her hair was pulled up high on her head, flowers gracing the tendrils. "What's this?" he asked, pulling out the one sheet of paper.

"This," she said, walking toward the table of men, "this is for you mostly, Vincent, but for every lost girl never found. I hope... I hope that in the future more are found than lost." She handed him the paper, and he sucked in a shuddering breath. "I hope that Isabella's House will be a beacon to all women trying to escape or find safety. We'll hire staff to manage the mansion in the Hampton's, but it will now be a safe house for battered, abused, or at-risk girls and women."

Vincent nodded, tears rolling down his weathered face. He stood and pulled Kat into a hug. The other men all threatened to spill tears as well. She'd known them since she was a child but never understood the term of Russian princess until now. She had enough wealth and real estate to be classified as a princess, a title she definitely did not want.

"Thank you, Katarina. Isabella would have loved this. I'll make sure that the Scalias oversee the running of the house." She nodded as the priest entered the restaurant. She and Whiskey spoke with him for a few minutes, signed the paperwork, and then turned to look at the room full of family and friends.

"Well, looks like it's time for me to get married," she said, smiling at Whiskey. He was dressed in a pair of dark dress pants and a light blue shirt, just the way she would want him – no ties, no jackets. Not for this man. She would have been happy to see him in his jeans or uniform, but he'd opted for something at least slightly dressy. He took his place next to the priest, Ghost on his left, while Grace stood on the other side. The room full of men sat in the chairs lined on each side, and at the end of the aisle, Kat slid her hand into George's bent arm.

"Thank you, George. Thank you for doing this for me," she whispered.

"My pleasure, Sunshine. You're going to be happy, Kat. You and that big, ugly asshole at the end of the aisle will have a lifetime of happiness. You hear me?" She nodded and kissed his cheek as he handed her off to Whiskey.

Thirty minutes later, she was Mrs. Wade English, wife, old lady, and multi-millionaire.

CHAPTER TWENTY-FIVE

"What do you mean there is no money in the accounts?" he asked the man standing in front of him. "I need the money in Katarina's accounts transferred to my accounts before she does anything foolish. Sell the houses. Sell the properties. I need that money."

"Sir, the money was transferred to an account in the name of Wade and Katarina English yesterday. The houses have all transferred title to..."

"TO WHO!?" he screamed.

"The... the horse farm went to Vincent Scalia. The property in San Francisco to Chan Wu. The castle in Ireland to Ian Laughlin, and the lands in Russia, all of it went to the Ivanov family." The accountant stepped back, knowing that this man was about to blow and blow big. Everything he'd hoped to have, the properties he needed to liquidate for cash, was now suddenly no longer available to him.

Anton turned, staring out the large expanse of windows toward the ice-filled Chesapeake. It was colder earlier than usual. Just like Russia, it was cold and suddenly desolate and empty. He had nothing. No fucking money, no property, and that little bitch was the one responsible for all of it. He would still kill her, but it wouldn't matter any longer. Everything would go to that behemoth biker. Even if he died, nothing would come to him. Nothing.

"Sir, sir, what do you want..." Anton turned and fired a single bullet into the head of his former accountant.

"Bury him," he said to one of his men. The man casually lifted the body over his shoulder and made his way out of the office. Anton turned to Dolf and stared at the man as if waiting for something to come to him.

"Find Katarina and bring her to me. I may not get my money, but I will have my fun." Dolf nodded, smiling at the man. "Yes, my big friend, you can have your fun as well." A low growl escaped from the big man as he turned and left his boss alone.

It was gone. Every penny was gone. If his men knew he had no money for payroll, they would leave him. He had a handful of loyal men here and in Russia, but they would only remain loyal for so long if he couldn't pay them.

Fucking little cunt! She'd been a thorn in his side since her birth. He wanted her dead at first, but when his wife convinced him that she would be good to use as a pawn eventually, he gave in. There had been glimpses of moments when he'd actually felt like her father, indulging her, allowing her the little girl fancies she desired. He should have killed her.

Now he was certain he would be facing the fucking bikers.

"My shipments," he whispered. "If I can get payment for my shipments, it will be a start. Yes, that's it. I can start over." He pulled out the folder and started adding the numbers. Seven shipments of drugs, three shipments of weapons, two shipments of women. Once paid, he would have a nice little nest egg to begin again. He could start here or move to Russia and begin again in the homeland.

Yes, that's what I'll do. I will rule again.

CHAPTER TWENTY-SIX

Grace, Bree, and Kat sat at the big kitchen table. George was leaning against the huge six-burner stove, his weathered hands folded on his chest. Ghost stood next to Whiskey, Ace, Zulu, and Gunner.

"We can't tell you everything that will happen in the next twenty-four hours. You know that, but our number one priority is keeping Kat safe until this is all over. Ace, Zulu, George, and Gunner will all be here to protect the three of you. Do everything, and I do mean everything, they say. Do I make myself clear to all of you?" Three heads nodded, and Ghost waited.

"Oh, umm, yes," said Bree.

"Yes, baby," said Grace, smiling at her husband. Ghost waited, staring at Kat.

"You can't expect me to just sit here and do nothing when it's my life hanging in the balance, Ghost." She folded her arms, and the others all groaned at her petulant behavior.

"Your life? Your life, Sunshine? That's my wife sitting next to you with my child! That's Doc's fiancée on the other side of you. Those men... those men standing in front of you are my brothers. The only family I've ever known. This is not just your life, Kat, not by a long shot." Kat swallowed, feeling the tears rise in her eyes. She expected Whiskey to comfort her, but he didn't. His silence only made her feel worse about her behavior.

"I... I'm sorry. You're right, of course. My apologies. I'll stay here with everyone. I'll do whatever they say." Ghost nodded at her and turned to the men.

"You'll take all three to the safe house. We stocked it just last week, so there's plenty of food and firewood. Try to avoid a fire if you can, so it won't be spotted. No one knows where it is. Cover the tracks. Lock down the restaurant. Put a sign on the door that there's a gas leak. Chain the gates, hide the bikes. Make it look like there's no one home because that's what we hope the bastards will think."

"Where will you be, Ghost?" asked Grace.

"Baby, I can't tell you everything, but just know that we're going to be ridding the ship of the rats. We'll be gone a few days, so don't panic if you don't hear from us right away. Just do as the boys say." Grace nodded, giving an instinctive rub to her belly. Ghost pulled her toward him, enveloping her in the comforting scents of leather and musk.

"I love you, Ghost," she whispered.

"I love you too, honey." He kissed her and left the room. Kat watched as Doc pulled Bree in for a tight hug, kissing her passionately. She heard their exchange of 'I love yous' and smiled. Whiskey walked toward her and pulled her into the hallway.

"Listen to everything they say, baby girl. They know what they're doing. Don't do anything stupid. You hear me?" She nodded, nibbling on her lower lip. "I love you, Mrs. English."

"I love you too, Mr. English," she said, smiling through the tears.

"Baby girl, don't cry, please. You're breakin' my heart here. I'll be back soon. I promise." She nodded and watched as he pulled away, following his brothers down the hall. She heard the slamming of the first steel door and then the second, jumping at the echo.

"Gather everything you might need for at least a week, ladies," said Gunner. "Zulu? Pull the Hummer up to the back. Ace? Gather any gear you'll need. Secure all the locks and gates." Ace nodded as Zulu disappeared out the back door.

Thirty minutes later, they were loaded into the white Hummer, its color camouflaging against the snow-covered fields. Kat wondered if they had one in every color of the seasons. They took the back farm roads, and thirty minutes later, they pulled up to a two-story log cabin. There was a wrap-around porch and stunning views of the mountains.

Looking at the front door, Kat wondered how the wooden structure would keep anyone out that wanted to get in, but when Zulu opened the door, she realized it was a steel door just like the ones at the club, simply painted to look like a wood door.

The open living space gave way to a large, well-equipped chef's kitchen and huge living room with a fireplace. There were four bedrooms, all with two sets of bunk beds to accommodate as many people as possible. The girls would all share one room upstairs. Downstairs, Ace would have his own room, Gunner and George sharing a room, and Zulu in his own room, the big man needing to shove two beds together in order to get any sleep.

By the time the bags were placed in the rooms, it was nearly supper time. George busied himself in the kitchen while the ladies talked about babies and weddings and Christmas. Ace sat somewhat apart from the group but watched in earnest, listening to the conversations. After dinner, they played a few games of trivial pursuit and then decided to turn in early.

In the darkness of the bedroom, Kat could hear the soft breathing of Grace and Bree, but sleep escaped her. The feeling of despair and panic enveloped her as she struggled to find a sliver of light in the room. Finally unable to take any more, she rose and went downstairs.

The light from the cloud-covered sky seeped through the upper windows of the vaulted room, just enough to let Kat breathe. She curled up on the sofa, wrapping the old quilt around her shoulders.

"It's just the dark. There's nothing there," she whispered. "It's just the dark…"

"Can't sleep?" She jumped, covering the scream threatening to escape. Seeing the tall, lean figure of Ace, she sat back down.

"I'm so sorry, Ace. Did I wake you?"

"Nah, I don't sleep much anyway," he said, sitting on the other sofa across from her. "I was monitoring the chatter from the teams." Kat waited with bated breath. "They're all fine. Things are going well."

"I hate the dark," she whispered. Ace nodded, understanding the feeling. "When my uncle locked me in the basement all those times, I would repeat those words to myself over and over again. It's just the dark. There's nothing there. I think I was just trying to convince myself of it, to be honest, but I learned to hate the dark, and he knew it."

Ace nodded his head again. There was something about this woman that made him feel like he could tell her everything.

"I hate the dark as well," he said quietly. Kat said nothing, hoping he would continue. She knew that he wouldn't if she jumped in. "It wasn't a basement for me. It was a closet. My foster parents caged me inside a closet."

Kat could feel the tears already falling down her cheeks but held in the need to sob for the man sitting across from her.

"From the time I was five years old to almost thirteen. When I was found, I was only sixty-eight pounds. Barely as big as a third-grader and barely able to read." He took a deep breath and stared out the windows at the moon as silvery clouds floated by. "I was never given clothes. I had a bucket to use as a bathroom. I was allowed one shower a month. I had one meal a day, if that's what you call it. But it was the hands between the bars. The hands..."

"Ace," she whispered, "you don't have to..."

"I think I do," he said quietly. "They would let their drunken friends into the bedroom. Allow them to reach through the bars and touch me, tease me, some pinched me, some… Those hands… those hands are all I see sometimes." Kat swallowed and nodded. She saw the same thing.

"My cousin, who I thought was my brother, he did the same thing when he was tormenting me. Reaching through the bars, grabbing at me, pinching me…" She shook her head, and Ace stared at the young woman. They weren't so very different after all.

"One night… one night, one of the couples my parents were partying with weren't so into torturing a child. They pretended but left and called the cops. By midnight, I was in a hospital under CPS care. One of the cops who rescued me refused to leave my side. He wanted to kill my foster parents on the spot but instead decided to foster me."

"He was the most patient, kind, decent man to have ever lived. He'd raised one son already, and he and his wife were divorced, but it didn't matter. He was more than enough. He changed my life. He was a Navy veteran and talked about his time in service a lot.

"He got me the best tutors, the best therapists, and within three years, I was at my grade level in school. I was still small but probably average to my classmates. When I went off to college, I had my first panic attack. Someone bumped into me in a crowded hallway. I went nuts. My foster dad pulled me out of college and let me complete my coursework at home. I had my degree within two years."

"Interviews were a nightmare. I mean, how do you start with 'sorry, I can't shake your hand. I'm mental.' I was out looking for work one day and passed by the recruiting office. I thought it might be right for me. I explained to the recruiter my condition, and he assured me they would make special considerations for me, given my IQ and skill set. They did, for the most part, but I was never able to sleep in the same space as the other guys."

"I'm so sorry, Ace," she said, lifting her hand to touch his arm. She pulled back, embarrassed that she'd already forgotten.

"It's okay, Kat. I mean, when we shook hands, I was okay." She nodded again and touched his arm lightly. She just let it sit there for a few seconds and then drew back. He waited for the panic to come, but when it didn't, he simply nodded.

"Go to sleep, Kat," he said, standing. "You're safe down here. We're all on this floor and will hear anything." She was already closing her eyes as he made his way toward the hallway. He nearly slammed right into the big body of Zulu, his midnight black face and eyes almost hidden in the shadows.

"I'm sorry, brother, real fucking sorry. I didn't mean to listen in. I won't tell the others." Zulu wanted to reach out and hug the younger man.

"It's okay, Zulu. I knew you were there. I could feel you," he said quietly. "Between you and me and Kat, yea?"

"Yea, brother. Between you and me and Kat." Zulu watched as the young man maneuvered around his body and closed the bedroom door. A few seconds later, he saw the light click on, the glow seeping from the bottom of the door.

CHAPTER TWENTY-SEVEN

Ghost and Whiskey huddled over the massive oak table in one of the mansions owned by Vincent Scalia. It was one of many, but this one was just outside of D.C. The raids on the shipments had gone off like clockwork. Money, guns, drugs, and women and children all recovered and stolen from Anton Krevnyv. He had to be panicking at this moment with nothing at his disposal.

"I just heard from Ian and Colin," said Vincent. "Colin and his team have decimated the crew in Boston. He's already on the private jet on his way back here. Ian wiped out the group in New York and New Jersey. Things went exactly as we predicted. Once his main teams started to fall, the others took off. Even the ones who didn't eventually left when they realized he had no resources, no money."

"Nice to know they have loyalty," said Ghost.

"Loyal or not, men still need to be paid," said Vincent. Ghost nodded, almost wanting to apologize to the man. He didn't mean to insult his profession, but then again, he was a mafia boss.

"What about the West Coast?" asked Whiskey.

"Wu's men from China are still fighting, but at this point, he says they're winning. The Russians have all but taken over their territory. Ivan is going to stay a few more days to make sure things are settled there." Whiskey nodded, looking at the map in front of them.

"We have to find him," said Whiskey. "Kat thought he was close, which would mean he's at the house in Chesapeake."

"Up for a drive, gentlemen?" asked Vincent. They both nodded as the man excused himself to change out of his custom-made suit. Fifteen minutes later, he was wearing black utility pants and a black utility sweater. Whiskey couldn't help but smile, seeing the designer label on both. At least he was trying.

"Tony? Sal? With me," he shouted to the two no-necked men at the door. They followed eagerly, jumping into the driver and passenger seat of the SUV.

"Weapons?" asked Whiskey.

"Trunk full, my friend. We're always prepared," he said, smiling. "Tony? Find the house in Chesapeake where Krevnyv is hiding." The big man nodded as they took off in the direction of the Chesapeake.

"He's my kill," said Vincent casually. Whiskey started to protest but then realized the man was right. He'd brutally murdered his daughter. He deserved this kill. He nodded at the older man, looking beside him at Ghost.

"I know you love Katarina. She's a special young woman. Just don't hurt her," he said, turning in his seat.

"I have no plans on hurting her, Vincent," said Whiskey, somewhat perturbed by the comment.

"We never plan on hurting the ones we love, Whiskey," he said, grinning. "Listen, I get that you've seen and done a lot in your life. So have I. War. Different kinds of war, but it's still war. Ripping apart families and neighborhoods, cities, and countries. It's all still war. Isabella, she was my only child. Her mother, Anna, God rest her soul, was the only woman I ever loved. We argued like a ref and boxer on fight night."

The men in the car all chuckled, and Vincent shook his head at the memories.

"She had a hot Italian temper and wasn't afraid to unleash it on me, but I always, always said 'I'm sorry.' Even when it wasn't my fault, I said I'm sorry." He looked off in the distance and then spoke again. "I've seen a lot in my life, Whiskey. I have a way of seeing, just knowing, and I can already see that Kat's money is going to be a sore spot for you."

Whiskey squirmed in his seat, wondering how the man had seen into his very soul. He had done nothing but think about the money since she'd gotten it. It was literally millions of dollars and property to which the likes of he had never seen. She could go off and do anything she wanted with her life. Anything. She didn't need to be strapped down to a broken Marine biker.

"I see your eyes, son. I hear your thoughts. You're coming up with all sorts of ways to push that girl away. Instead of doing that, why don't you think of all the reasons you want to hold her close. Never let her go. That's where the love comes in Whiskey. Not the pushing away. The pushing away is easy. It makes everything easier, simpler. The holding close? Man, that's when you feel it. When you know the love of the woman is yours and yours alone."

Whiskey thought about the man's words for a moment, letting them sink in. He saw Ghost beside him mulling over the speech as well.

"I... I'm not good enough for her," he said quietly.

"Bullshit! That's a fucking cowardly statement to make. You're perfect for her. She needed someone strong, full of willpower, mature, worldly. She didn't need some piss-ant college student drinking fruity cocktails and foamy lattes. She needed a man, and you are it.

"Let me ask you something, Whiskey," he said, staring at the man, "if something were to happen to her, if you went back to the safe house tomorrow, and she was gone, or worse, what would that feel like?"

Whiskey felt the pain twisting in his chest, like a hot knife carving him from the inside out, his heart beating so fast he thought he would explode. He touched his chest and rubbed it, breathing heavily, sweat beading on his forehead.

"I think that answers my question," said Vincent. "Love her, Whiskey. Love her and invite me to dinner once in a while." The older man turned, smiling, to stare out the windshield. He spoke casually to Tony and Sal, directing them down the road.

"What about that, brother?" said Ghost, smiling. "You just got marriage advice from the biggest mob boss in the world."

CHAPTER TWENTY-EIGHT

Hawk and Eagle perched on the top of the building in South Boston, waiting for Colin's word. They knew Krevnyv's men were headed this way, but they wanted to make sure the streets were cleared. Colin's team had gone door to door telling people to stay inside. Now it was just a waiting game. A fucking cold waiting game, but a waiting game none the less.

"Rounding the corner now," said Colin in their earpiece. Eagle looked at Hawk, nodding to the right, and Hawk nodded to his left. They would take them out with ease from this angle. As the first of the men exited the SUVs, Eagle took aim. Taking in a deep breath, he relaxed and began the prayer that he and his brother had said a hundred times when on foreign soil.

"Father, forgive us for what we are about to do. We do not want to take the life that is yours. We only wish to save a life worth saving. We hope you make our aim true, our hearts pure, and our souls untarnished. We pray for your forgiveness. Amen." Their voices in unison ended the prayer, and both men fired, taking out all six men in each SUV.

"Fecking hell, that was lovely, boys," said the voice of Colin. "As a good Irish Catholic boy, I appreciated the prayer as well. I may have to use that if you don't mind." Eagle smiled at his brother.

"I don't mind," said Eagle into the mic. "We're Irish Catholics ourselves, so consider it a brotherly gift." They could hear the laughter of Colin on the other end and smiled as they headed downstairs to meet him. Stepping into the SUV, Colin laughed at them both.

"Let's go, boyos. We're headed back to D.C. to help."

"What about your brothers in New York and New Jersey? Are we needed there?" asked Hawk.

"Blood thirsty?" he asked, raising a brow.

"Nah, but that was fun. Fucking fat cats could barely reach their weapons when they realized the others were falling. They weren't even hard targets."

"Sorry to disappoint, lads," said Colin. "Let's pray that we have a boring trip back." Hawk and Eagle knew they should be grateful for the ease of the mission, but they enjoyed their jobs a little too much sometimes. Colin could be heard speaking to several men on the phone, hanging up, and immediately dialing the next. Turning in the seat, he spoke to the twins.

"They're all down, every last cowardly one of them. Vincent and yer men are headed to the Russian in Chesapeake. We'll meet them there if necessary or head to the club. The women are in safe keepin' somewhere." Eagle nodded, praying they were indeed safe. If anything happened to Grace, Bree, or Kat, the men wouldn't be consolable.

CHAPTER TWENTY-NINE

"That's the house, boss," said Tony, pointing at the big white mansion on the bay. There were two cars in the circular drive, but ideally, there should have been a dozen to protect the man. Twilight was settling over the bay, and the dark, clouded sky would help them blend in. The tall reeds on the side of the driveway gave them adequate coverage. No cameras were spotted, but that didn't mean they weren't there, and Whiskey was careful to search for motion detectors or tripwires.

"Tony? You and Sal take the back of the house facing the water. Make sure he doesn't try to head out by boat. We'll take the front door." Sal held up a thermal scanner and moved slowly from one side of the house to the other. Whiskey raised an impressed eyebrow, and Ghost chuckled beside him.

"Nice equipment," said Ghost.

"Only the best, my friend," he smiled.

"I see only three men, sir," said Sal. "Two in the library. My guess is it's him and one other. There's one in the kitchen. I'll take that one through the back door. If I see any others, I'll signal." Sal took off down the worn path toward the house, his movements easy and sure for such a large man.

"He trained?" asked Ghost, admiring the movements.

"All my men are trained, Ghost, but yes, Sal served in the Army for ten years before coming under my employ. He left the service and couldn't find work. I saw his abilities as an asset and hired him immediately. He's the best, he and Tony both."

"Let's go," said Whiskey. As they reached the front door, Whiskey easily picked the lock and opened it to find no one waiting for them and no alarm on. Was this idiot that much of a narcissist, or did he forget to pay the bills? It was almost a disappointment. He heard voices down the left hallway and motioned for the two men to follow. As they moved closer, they heard the voice of Sal in their ears, confirming they'd neutralized the man in the kitchen. So far, no others were in sight.

Whiskey stood outside the office door listening to Krevnyv in a panicked voice, yelling at the man in front of him. Where were his men? Where were his shipments? When would he have access to more money? He was utterly panicked and out of control.

Whiskey pushed the door open, leveling his weapon at the head of Anton Krevnyv. He didn't even appear surprised.

"I should have killed you when I had the chance," he snarled at Whiskey. Following Whiskey, Ghost took the weapon of the second man, shoving him to the floor, zip tying his hands. Behind him, Vincent stepped into the office. Krevnyv's face turned white as he sat back in the office chair.

"Vince... Vincent... we can talk about this, Vincent. It's my daughter... my fucking daughter..." Whiskey delivered a hard punch to the side of his head, his ears ringing, his vision blurred.

"Don't speak of your *niece,* you sick fuck. Don't you speak of my wife!"

"You... you're Wade English? You piece of shit! You fucking piece of shit! You're nothing but a low-life fucking biker. Do you really think she'll want you? Did you really believe she would stay married to you? That slut! You've ruined everything... everything I had planned..."

"You killed my daughter," said Vincent quietly. Krevnyv stopped his tirade directed at Whiskey and swallowed.

"Vince... it was a misunderstanding... Dolf, he got carried away..."

"Don't you dare speak of her. Don't you dare give me your excuses, you twisted mental patient. You know, in the old days, Anton, we would hang you upside down, cut out your tongue, and then skin you alive. I wish I had the patience for that today. I truly wish I did. But you're not going to get that death. You're going to get a quick one. Something you don't deserve."

"You can die knowing Katarina will live a happy life. She'll grow old and have babies and enjoy the money you stole from her." Krevnyv smiled and then laughed at the man.

"You fool," he laughed, "she won't live a happy life... she won't live any life. She will die miserably just like Isabella... Dolf will make sure of it..." he laughed a sinister sound, making chills run up Whiskey's back.

"What the fuck are you talking about?" he asked, gripping the man by the throat.

"He's already there... he'll have so much fun... so much..." He didn't finish the sentence as Vincent's bullet went through his forehead. Whiskey looked at him pleadingly.

"We don't have time for games, unfortunately. We have to get to Kat. Call your men. Call them now. Let them know that Dolf is on his way." He knelt next to the man on the floor, gripping his hair in his hands. "How many men are with Dolf?" The man said nothing, and he slammed his face into the tiled floor.

"I won't ask again. This can be a quick death or slow. How many?"

"None, it's just... it's just Dolf... that's all he would need..." Another bullet, another dead Russian.

"Let's go."

"They're not answering," said Ghost, feeling panicked. "Tell us everything you know about Dolf." They raced toward the SUV, Tony and Sal already seated, ready to drive. They'd contacted Colin to tell him to head toward the club and safe house with the twins.

"Dolf has been with Anton for years now. He was a Russian powerlifter at one time, kicked out of the Olympics for drug use. He's massive. Your friend Zulu is tiny compared to Dolf. I think he continues to take steroids; he's so big and beyond strong and angry all the time. He's also sick in the head. He kills not because it's his job but because it gives him pleasure. He tortures women, beyond tortures them. I've often wondered if he were not human."

"Jesus," whispered Ghost, dialing the number again.

"Pray to him and anyone else you can think of. Anton was vicious, but this man is psychotic and will enjoy taking Kat. He's been obsessed with her for years and wanted her as his own."

Whiskey was falling apart. He could feel it, the panic in his chest, the tears welling in his eyes. They were at least two hours away, and they couldn't reach the men on the phone. Either the reception was bad, or Dolf was already there.

"Their bracelets," said Ghost, staring at his friend. "Check the app, the beacons..." Whiskey opened the app and breathed a sigh of relief. The three dots were all together, exactly where the safe house should be.

"Okay, okay, we're good for now. Let's just get there and stop this before that man gets to your girl," said Vincent.

CHAPTER THIRTY

George continued to put the dishes away, watching the front of the property, waiting for Gunner to return. Turning off the kitchen light, he sat next to the three women on the sofa and looked over at Zulu, who had the same expression of concern on his face.

Ace walked from the back bedrooms and nodded at Zulu, who stood to meet the man.

"Comms are down," he whispered. "Something is interfering in the signal. I'm working on it, but someone is jamming our communication. Get the women in the basement, brother. Get them out of here." Zulu nodded, looking back at the women.

"Ladies," he said calmly and quietly, "I need you to calmly get up and get your jackets and shoes on." Kat's face blanched, and Grace immediately gripped her stomach. "Calmly, ladies. George, you'll go with them." The women casually pulled on their boots and grabbed their jackets. Zulu opened the door to the basement and turned on the light. Kat immediately stepped back.

"I know, beautiful. I know, but you have to trust me," said Zulu. She looked up at the giant, his dark eyes filled with compassion and worry. "I promise it will be okay."

"We're together, Kat," said Bree, "that's all that matters. We're together." She squeezed the younger woman's hand and pulled her toward the steps. Zulu guided the women downstairs and then opened another large steel door hidden behind a shelf. A long tunnel stood before them.

"A... a tunnel," said Kat in a whisper, "I... I can't... I..."

"You can, Sunshine," said Zulu, "you have to. George is going with you. He'll be with you the whole way. The tunnel is a shortcut back to the property. It will take you about twenty minutes to walk it, but you'll come right back up in our cellar there. There's a huge locker with ammunition and guns. George will open it. Take what you can and use it. Do you hear me?"

"I hear you," said Grace.

"I hear you," said Bree.

"Sunshine? I need to hear the words," he said, gripping the upper arms of Kat.

"I... I hear you... I... hear you..." she whispered.

"Grace? Take this," he said, thrusting the pistol into her hand. "Shoot if you have to. Understand?" She nodded.

"I understand."

"Good." He looked at the three women, and his heart twisted in his chest. Pulling each one close, he kissed their foreheads and shoved them toward the tunnel. George stepped in with a flashlight and shut the big door behind him. Zulu pushed the shelf back in place and then grabbed his own service weapons, one in each hand.

Taking the steps slowly, he entered the hallway to find Ace standing, just listening. He pointed toward the back door, and Zulu nodded. Moving toward the door, he saw a large figure through the glass and opened the door swiftly, pulling in the bloody body of Gunner.

"Fuck," he growled, shutting the door and locking it. "Brother, Gunner, talk to me, man."

"Big... big fucker... bigger than you..."

"Only one?" asked Zulu. Gunner nodded, wincing as he did so. Only one? Zulu shook his head. If they only sent one, he was either some sort of Special Forces soldier or just an everyday killing machine. Ace reached for Gunner and felt around his head, his eyes wide with shock. His hands shook as he touched his brother, but he knew he had to do this.

"Ace?" whispered Zulu. Ace shook his head.

"It's okay... it's okay... he won't hurt me... he won't hurt me... h-he has a head injury, nothing else from the looks of it." He pulled his hands away and wiped them roughly on the front of his jeans.

"Let's get him to the back room." Zulu lifted Gunner under one arm and moved quickly to lie him on the bed in the back. "Can you see, Gunner?"

"Yea, if I'm still, my vision is clear." He handed him two weapons and propped him against the pillows on the bed.

"Shoot if anyone comes through here. We'll tell you if it's one of us."

"The girls... the girls..." he whispered.

"Gone." Gunner gave a small nod and held the weapons at his side. "Zulu? He's a big fucker, bigger than you, and strong. I've never felt anything like it in my life."

Zulu nodded once again and headed back toward the living room. At first, he didn't see Ace, but as his vision adjusted to the light in the room, he spotted the large, shadowed figure holding Ace by the throat. Zulu fired a round into his shoulder. Nothing. Again. The body of Ace fell to the floor, coughing.

That's when Zulu saw it – the look of death of the man's face. He turned, staring at Zulu as if he were a fly to be squashed. The Russian looked him up and down as if to size up his opponent. Zulu knew that feeling. He was doing the same damn thing. This was the biggest motherfucker he'd ever seen in his life.

Zulu was six-foot-six and two hundred and eighty pounds of muscle. This guy easily had three inches on him and thirty pounds. But it was the thickness of his hands and fingers, the pure strength radiating from his limbs that had Zulu worried. He'd fired two bullets into his hide, and the man was still standing.

Ace, still crumpled on the floor, was gasping for air, his windpipe no doubt crushed or damaged.

"Where is Katarina?" he asked in a heavily accented voice.

"Gone, big man. Gone." Zulu tried to distract him, getting him to talk as long as he could. If he could give George some extra time, then they would be safe and locked in at the barn by the time this guy tried to get to them.

"You lie. Where is my ballerina?"

Christ! Thought Zulu. He sounds like the slow dude from the book *Of Mice and Men*. He's truly off his fucking rocker, and I'm not sure what will stop him.

"Sorry, man, not lying. She's gone. We put her on a plane earlier today and sent her west." The big man looked at Zulu, rage filling his body.

"No! She is mine. I was promised by boss. She is mine!" he took a step toward Zulu, and he held up both weapons. The big man stopped, staring at him. "I will tear her apart. I will feel her bleed on me like other women, but I will save her for a long time."

"Okay, fucker, you gotta die," said Zulu, unloading his weapon into the man. He realized too late he was wearing upper body armor. Firing again, he put two in his right leg and a third in his left leg. He fell but immediately stood coming at Zulu again. Zulu continued to fire until his weapon was empty. The big man lunged for him, and Zulu dodged to the side.

"You're hit, big guy. Let's get you to a doctor," said Zulu, trying to placate the beast.

"I want my ballerina," he said, growling. He dove for Zulu, catching him against his chest and squeezing. Zulu squirmed, trying to put space between him and the other man. He lifted him off the floor, swinging him like a rag doll.

What the fucking hell? I'm off the floor!

Zulu pushed his arms beneath the giant's and tried to break free. He squeezed tighter and tighter, the air leaving his lungs a little at a time.

"I want my ballerina!" he yelled.

"No... can... do," gasped Zulu.

"Let him go!" Zulu collapsed to the floor, his lungs gasping for air. At first, he wasn't sure where the sound had come from, and then he turned to see Kat standing on the other side of the room. "Let them all go, and I'll go with you, Dolf. Don't hurt them. They're my friends."

CHAPTER THIRTY-ONE

Ghost, Whiskey, and Vincent stormed inside the club, searching each room, only to find nothing. They had to still be at the safe house. Running toward the basement, they froze at the top of stairs, hearing the commotion below. Whiskey turned on the light and slowly walked down the steps only to be greeted by George holding a pistol to his face.

"Fucking hell," whispered George dropping the weapon.

"Where's Kat?" screamed Whiskey. "Where is Kat?"

"She took off back toward the house," said George. "She panicked in the tunnel and couldn't take it. She took off so quickly. I had to make a choice, Whiskey. I had to get Grace and Bree to safety."

Whiskey nodded, angry at first but knowing it was the right thing to do. From behind them, they heard more footsteps and turned to see Eagle, Hawk, and Colin.

"She went back," squeaked Whiskey in desperation and panic.

"Let's go, brother," said Hawk, pulling him with him. "We'll take the SUV. Colin? Follow my brother through the tunnel. Run!"

Colin took off like a shot through the dark tunnel. Eagle kept a good pace behind him, but he wasn't used to doing the training miles that an MMA fighter would do. He was fast, no doubt could outrun most on his team, but Colin was at a whole other level.

"How far?" he called back.

"About fifteen-minute brisk walk. If we run, we cut it to seven or eight minutes," said Eagle.

"Bollucks, let's make it six…" He took off at a pace that even Eagle couldn't keep up with, but he knew he would be right behind him. A few minutes later, Eagle could hear the big steel door at the end of the tunnel open and knew Colin had made it.

Taking the steps carefully, he heard the voices upstairs. As he got closer, he heard the soft voice of Kat trying to keep someone calm and the more urgent voices of two males. He inched his way along the hallway and spotted Gunner crumpled to the floor, blood oozing from a head wound, two guns gripped tightly in his hands, but obviously no clear shot at whomever he was aiming.

"Let the girl go, man," said Zulu. He knew it was the big man he'd met a few days ago and thought the other guy must be shitting his pants right about now. "You got nowhere to go."

"The ballerina is mine," said the big bass voice.

Oh fuuuuuckkk! It was the psycho, Dolf. Shit. Shit. Shit. Colin ran the scenario through his head a dozen times and knew he only had one choice to make. Okay, here goes nothing.

"Hello, ya big eedjit," said Colin, coming around the corner. He let out a breath, realizing the big man didn't have a weapon. Only Kat pressed against his chest like he had an infant in a carrier. He was bleeding from a few holes, but it would take a lot more to bring him down.

"Don't call me that!" he yelled. Kat winced at the loudness of his voice.

"Yer hurtin' the lass, ya eedjit. If yer itchin' fer a fight, come along then," said Colin, standing straight.

"You're tricking me," said Dolf, eyeing the big Irishman.

"Nah, ye eedjit, I'm just tryin' to get ye to put the lass down, so she can catch her breath. Ye don't wanna kill her before ye have yer fun, do ya? I mean, ye could have a round or two with me and then run off with her." Kat's eyes went wide. She knew what Colin was trying to do, but Dolf would kill him. Zulu was still gasping for air as he reached for the big man's legs. Dolf swung a big foot back, connecting with Zulu square in the face, knocking him back. His vision was blurred, blood spurting from his nose as he tried to reach out again.

"Come on, ye big eedjit. Let's go," said Colin, taking another step forward. He saw Eagle from the corner of his eye, and signaling behind his back. He tried to get him to move out back to get a shot from behind.

"Fine. I fight the ugly orange hair, and then I take my ballerina." He literally tossed Kat like a piece of trash behind him. She landed on top of Zulu, who immediately pushed her behind him, his chest still pained. Ace scooted closer, wheezing with every movement.

"Thas right, big fella. Let's go," said Colin. The big man rushed toward Colin, and he swerved, avoiding the big body, tripping him as he moved past him. He fell hard to the wood floor and cursed in Russian but bounced up, growling like an angry bear, and Colin laughed at him.

Zulu watched the fight play out and thought Colin was about the stupidest fuck he'd ever met. The big man ran at him, and like a bullfighter, Colin dodged him once more. Leaping to the back of the sofa, he crawled up the man's back and wrapped his legs around his thick neck, squeezing with all his might as he jerked his jaw backwards. It was like trying to move a concrete barrier.

Dolf gripped the man's legs and, with great effort, forced them apart and tossed him against the wall near Zulu.

"I may need a different tactic," he said, grinning at Zulu.

"You're an idiot," he said, wheezing. "Grab a gun... headshot... only... way..."

"Aye, I'm gettin' there, big fella," he said, standing. He danced away from Zulu, Ace, and Kat, not wanting Dolf to get anywhere near them. He caught the glint of a red dot from the window and knew Eagle was in place.

"Time to take a nappie, big man," said Colin. He dove, flattening his body against the floor as glass shattered around them. Standing, he looked up to see the big man still standing. A bright red spot in the center of his head.

"Fecking hell," he whispered. It seemed like minutes before Eagle fired again, but seconds later, another bullet shattered through the glass, this time taking off the top of his head. He toppled to the floor, a loud thud echoing in the room as Colin leaned against the wall staring at the giant. The front door crashed open, and Whiskey, Ghost, and Vincent stormed in.

"Fuck! Is everyone okay?" yelled Ghost.

"Wh-whisky?" came the small voice from somewhere in the room.

"Kat? Kat, where are you?" he yelled, flipping on the lights.

"H-here... behind Zulu and Ace... help them... they're hurt. Gunner... Gunner is in the hallway," she cried. Whiskey knelt down and tried to pull Kat free, but Zulu and Ace had their bodies wedged in such a way that she couldn't get out, and they were too injured to move quickly.

"I-I'm okay... just help them," she said. Doc came through the door with his kit and knelt beside Gunner first. Next came Bree, and she moved toward Zulu.

"We need an ambulance," said Bree, calling over her shoulder.

"We can't, Bree," said Ghost. She shot him a look that had him stepping back for a moment, and then she nodded.

"Fine, but I need help getting Zulu up and back to the club." Colin stood and hobbled toward the big man.

"I'll help the big man. Fecking monster ye are," he said, grinning. "But that beastie was more than either of us could take down."

Zulu grinned and leaned on the big Irishman's shoulders, walking toward the car. Gunner was being bandaged by Doc. Whiskey leaned down to look at Ace, the purple and red marks around his throat telling him what he needed to know. He was gasping for air, his breathing labored. His face was ghostly white.

"Doc! You need to get over here now." Ghost took over for Doc, wrapping Gunner's head while he ran to Ace.

"Shit! I think his windpipe is crushed. Lay him down. I need light," he yelled behind him. Four men shone their flashlights directly on Ace as Kat scooted out of the corner into Vincent's arms. He hugged the girl tightly, kissing her head.

"You're going to have to answer to your husband for what you did, Kat," he said. Whiskey looked back with anger flashing in his eyes, and she nodded, tears flowing down her cheeks.

"Just... just save him... save Ace... he saved me... they all did..." She knelt beside Ace and held out her hand to him. Shocking them all, Ace gripped her hand tightly as Doc opened his trachea and placed the tube expertly in the hole. Immediately his breathing evened out, and his color began to return.

"Alright, we need to lift him carefully," said Doc, looking at the men around the room.

"I'm sorry, Ace," she whispered, "I'm sorry... I couldn't... the dark... the dark..." He only nodded, a tear slipping down his cheek. Kat released his hand and knelt on the glass-covered floor, sobbing into her hands. The men walked out one by one, except Whiskey, who carefully picked her up and held her against his chest.

"I know, baby girl. I know," he whispered.

"I'm sorry... I'm so sorry... I'm such a mess... I'm not worth it, Whiskey... I'm not worth it..." He sat on the sofa, rocking her back and forth. Kissing the side of her face, he just held her until the tears stopped.

"Listen to me, baby. Are you listening?" he asked. She nodded, looking up at him with swollen eyes and lips. "You are worth everything. Every fucking thing. Now, am I mad about what you did? Yea, I'm fucking flaming mad, baby. You risked your life and the lives of my brothers instead of trusting in George to get you to safety. We're gonna get you some help for the panic attacks, babe, but that one almost cost me three brothers and you."

"I'm s-sorry," she stuttered.

"I know you are, Kat. I know, baby. And I know how hard that must have been for you. But I needed you to trust George. Trust me and these men to keep you safe. Do you understand what Dolf would have done to you if he'd taken you?" She nodded.

"Okay, let's get back and make sure the boys are okay."

"H-how are we getting back?" she asked.

"I'm taking you for a walk, baby." Her eyes grew wide, and she started to shake. "Do you trust me, Kat?" She nodded. "Then trust that all will be well. We're going to walk back home, and you're going to see that there is nothing to be afraid of in the dark. Nothing, baby girl."

Kat did as he asked, following him downstairs and back through the tunnel. This time there wasn't even the light of George's flashlight. Only darkness. She gripped his hand so tightly that twice, he had to switch hands so his fingers wouldn't go numb. He spoke to her the entire time, pulling her with him. The fifteen-minute walk ended up taking almost thirty minutes, but when they reached the other end, she took a deep, shuddering breath and dropped to her knees, crying again.

"Come on, baby girl. Let's get you cleaned up," he said, lifting her.

"N-no, I need to see Ace, Zulu, and Gunner. I need to make sure they're okay," she sobbed.

"After, baby, after."

CHAPTER THIRTY-TWO

Vincent and Colin stayed by the men's sides, helping Doc and Bree where they could. Colin had experienced enough injuries in his career to know exactly what to do for a concussion, contusions, broken bones, and cuts. He helped most with Gunner, having had a few head injuries himself, but once he was settled, he moved toward Zulu.

"How are ye, big man?" he asked, smiling down at the large black man. His biceps bulged with rippling muscles, his chest and abdomen revealing an eight-pack instead of a six-pack. Colin thought he'd hate to meet up with this beast in the ring.

"Are you always so fucking happy, Irish?" he asked, grinning at the big redhead.

"Aye, I suppose I am. Nothin' to be sad about. We took down the jolly Russian giant, my friend. I'd say that's for the record books. That arsehole is known for taking horse steroids to improve his performance. Judging by the way he took us out, I'd say he was takin' double doses for sure."

"Yea, it sure as fuck felt that way. I've met a lot of big men in my time. They always seem to want to challenge the other big guy in the room. I've been through BUD/s, been a SEAL, and fucking trained with the best. That dude, that fucker was beyond strong, man. I felt my rips crack in one squeeze." Colin nodded, looking soberly at his friend.

"Aye, and ken you imagine if he'd gotten a hold of our Kat?" he said, grimacing. Zulu could only nod.

"How are Gunner and Ace?" he asked Colin.

"Aye, yer man Gunner's got a right hard head, he has. Fecker must be Irish," he grinned. "The wee lad, Ace, he's a tube in his neck, but yer Doc says he'll be fine." Zulu frowned but nodded.

"You know, he's not really a wee lad," said Zulu in his best Irish accent. "He's smaller than us, but he's a solid six foot and two bills." Colin chuckled and nodded. "What about Kat? Where is she?"

"Ah, well, her husband has her locked up right now. No tellin' what he's sayin'." Zulu nodded again.

"I can't even imagine how frightened of the dark she must have been to run back toward the mess. I mean, she had to have been easily halfway home when she turned around. Poor George must have been so torn to have to make the decision to continue with Bree and Grace." Colin nodded again, looking back toward the door.

"Aye, he's right torn about that," he said. "Worried yer friend, Whiskey, will be angry with him."

"Nah," said Zulu, "Whiskey won't be angry with him. He knows. What about you? You headed back to Boston?"

"Aye, the jet's bein' fueled now, and I'm headed to see me brother. Then we're off to spend some time in our newly retrieved castle," he said, grinning.

"Good luck, man," said Zulu, gripping his hand. "You were a fine fuck to fight with. That's for sure."

"So were you, big man, so were you. I'd be proud to fight with ye again if you ever need me help." Zulu nodded at him, laughing and then wincing, realizing how bad that hurt.

"I'll keep that mind. Stay safe, Colin." The Irishman smiled at him and turned to leave. He stopped briefly in the hallway to chat with Vincent, shaking his hand and then Ghost's as well. Walking into his room was Kat. Her face was red and puffy. Her eyes just slits on her face.

"A-are you okay?" she asked, standing in the door.

"Come here, Sunshine," said Zulu. "Don't be afraid. Come here." He patted the spot next to him on the bed, and she sat down, gripping his huge hand.

"I'm sorry, Zulu... I..." He held up a hand and smiled at her.

"I'm sure you don't need me to tell you how foolish that was. I'm sure your husband has laid into you big time. But listen, Kat, the risk to me, the risk to my brothers, that's all something we signed up for. But risking your life with that man? That was insanity. All because you can't cope with the dark? Honey, they have meds for that," he said with a grin. "Listen, I'm not making light of your fear. On the contrary, I can only imagine how terrified you must have been to turn back like that."

"I-I know... I... Whiskey is going to get me some help through Bree. I can't risk any of you... I can't risk me like that again. I'm so sorry, Zulu," she said with a sob wrapping her arms around his shoulders.

"I know, Sunshine. I know. I'm gonna be okay, so is Ace and Gunner. We'll all be okay now. Now you can focus on what you want to do. You can take the bar exam. You can start Isabella's House. You can do anything you want to do." She nodded and stood from the edge of the bed.

"Thank you, Zulu. Thank you for making sure I have a life to move on with." He smiled at her and leaned his head against the wall. He heard her move across the hall talking to Gunner and then looked up to see Whiskey's face. "Hey, brother. I..."

"Don't, man. Just fucking don't. I owe you my life, brother. My fucking life for saving that woman," he said.

"Listen, it was as much Colin and Ace as me. Gunner got whacked while on patrol, could have fucking died, but Ace? Man, that little shit took that big bastard on himself without thinking. He touched him, brother, touched him to save me." Whiskey nodded, looking back over his shoulder across the hall at Ace's room where Doc was still working on him.

"Maybe we get Bree to give him and Kat a two for one," he smiled. Zulu chuckled. "Get some sleep, man, if you can. Are the dreams better?" Zulu shrugged.

"Same. Always the same." Whiskey nodded and left the room, closing the door quietly behind him. He stepped across the hall and stood over Ace.

"Will he be okay, Doc?" he asked. Kat sat beside him, Ace's hand still holding hers. He couldn't believe it, couldn't fucking believe she'd gotten Ace to touch someone. He partly was pissed that he was touching her but partly pleased that his girl was able to make that happen.

"Windpipe wasn't crushed, but damaged, badly bruised. He won't be able to speak for a while but should be okay in a few weeks. I'm going to watch him tonight and then maybe take out the tube in the morning." Whiskey nodded and reached for Kat's hand. She gave a quick squeeze to Ace's hand and nodded at him.

It was nearly morning, and everyone was exhausted. Catching a few hours' sleep, they woke the next day to a huge breakfast by George. Kat walked in and immediately fell into the man's arms.

"I'm sorry, George. I'm so sorry I put you in that position," she said against his chest.

"Don't be sorry, honey. I was just so worried for you and the other girls, I didn't know what to do. Don't like to have to choose like that." She nodded and pushed back.

"I promise, I'm going to get help from Bree for it," she said. He smiled at her and turned back to his pancakes. The girls sat eating and chatting while the men excused themselves for a meeting.

With everyone back from the different parts of the country, they met in the large meeting room and waited until Vincent, Ian, and Wu were on the lines.

"Gentlemen," said Wu, "you kept your end of the bargain. Krevnyv is gone; his business is done, and we have our territories back. We owe you a debt."

"We're even," said Ghost. "Katarina is safe and, for now at least, there are no children being trafficked."

"We give you our word that none of our families will partake in such business," said Wu. "Ivanov has agreed that he will stop all trafficking on his end as well."

"That's good to hear. Ian? We can't thank you enough for lending us Colin. He was invaluable in bringing down Dolf. I have three men and Kat who wouldn't have survived without him and my sniper."

"Aye, he said he had a grand time with your team, Ghost," he laughed. "I believe my brother might like to join your merry men when he retires. He has my blessing."

"He'd be more than welcome on this team, Ian. Vincent, we hope to see you for Christmas dinner," said Whiskey.

"I will be there, Whiskey, and I hope you didn't spank Katarina too hard," he laughed.

"I don't think I'll share that type of information about my wife and I," said Whiskey. "What I will tell you is that we're getting her the help she needs so that this never happens again."

"I'm thrilled to hear that. Gentlemen? It's been a pleasure. I know the families on this call appreciate what you've done. We are going to try to work more effectively together in the future to prevent anything like this from happening again. Have a wonderful holiday, everyone!"

The call disconnected, and all the men sat silently, looking from one to the other. Eagle started to laugh, and Hawk soon followed. Within minutes they were all laughing.

"Weirdest fucking shit ever!" said Ghost.

CHAPTER THIRTY-THREE

The restaurant re-opened the following day to a full house. It was just five days until Christmas, and the women were scrambling to buy gifts. They left on their shopping excursion with Ice and Axe in tow, spending hours trying to find exactly what they wanted for each man.

Kat discovered that shopping with an endless wallet was one of the best things ever. She tried not to go overboard and, in the end, decided on the perfect gift for each man. As they walked into the clubhouse, Hawk was behind the bar when the phone rang.

"Club Steel, this is Hawk," he said.

"May I speak with Quincy?" said the voice on the phone.

"Quincy? Oh, wait, you mean Zulu. He's not feeling well. Can I take a message?"

"Will you tell him Gabi called, and I need help?"

"Sure. Can I help you in some way? Hello? Guess not," he said to no one.

Grace, Kat, and Bree made their way to the big meeting room and spread the gifts out along with all the wrapping paper and ribbon. For the next five hours, they boxed, wrapped, taped, tied, and bowed everything that passed through their hands, laughing and drinking as they did. Grace had non-alcoholic cider, but the other two drank more eggnog than they should have.

By seven o'clock, the men sought them out for dinner and happily helped them arrange the gifts under the tree.

"I've never seen so many wrapped presents in my life," said Eagle.

"Me either," said Hawk.

"We're twins, you fucking moron! If I saw it, chances are you saw it. God, you're such an idiot sometimes," he muttered as he walked away. Ghost shook his head and smiled at Grace and her belly. He would have a son soon. One that might act just like that. Lord, help him.

Whiskey found Kat at the table with the others, quietly eating. She smiled at them and laughed, and his heart knew she'd found her new home. She was seeing Bree every other day to cope with her fears, and he was certain she would overcome them at some point.

"I was wondering, Ghost," she said, staring at her husband's friend. "I was wondering with all the guys getting hurt here recently, mostly because of me, umm, would a clinic on-site be helpful for Doc?"

"It's a good idea, Kat," he said, nodding, "but Doc isn't an MD. We'd need to have a licensed physician to oversee the clinic, and we'd most likely have to open it to the public. It's a huge expense considering all the things we would need to open something like that." She nodded, her thoughts wandering.

"What are you thinking, baby girl?" asked Whiskey.

"Well, I was just thinking it's the perfect thing for me to fund. I mean, I could write it off if we offered it as a free community clinic. There's plenty to fund something like for a long time."

"I think it's fucking generous of you, Kat," said Gunner, his head still bandaged, "but like Ghost said, we'd need an MD and a lot of bullshit licensing to go along with it. If we can figure it out, though, no doubt we'd keep it in business, and Doc would have somewhere to work other than the back rooms."

"Can I ask... can I ask a question about... about what happened?" she said quietly, staring at Ghost.

"You can ask, Kat. I may not answer, but you can ask."

"My uncle, is he gone?" Ghost gave a quick nod. "And... and Dolf? He's really gone?" Again, a quick nod, and she let out a long breath. "Thank you." She stood and headed to the back where Whiskey was certain she would visit Zulu and Ace.

"Someone gonna tell me how she got Ace to touch her hand?" asked Razor.

"Not sure, brother," said Whiskey. "When we got to the house and were trying to work on Ace, he reached for her hand. Strangest fucking thing I've ever seen. Honestly thought I would blow a gasket at first, but it's Ace, you know? The brother who touches no one. I was shocked, and then he did it again when we got him back here. I think he and Kat may have some things in common. Maybe it's a first step for him."

All the men nodded, not saying anything.

"All I know is it took five of us to lift that big Russian fucker out of the house," said Blade. "I've never in my life seen anyone so big. I mean, Zulu is a big fuck, and I've had to support him a time or two, but that dude? Fucker was a giant. A dead giant, but still a giant."

"Yea, let's hope he doesn't have any brothers," said Ghost.

"Fuck, with my luck, he'd have a sister," said Blade. The table exploded with laughter as they finished their meal. An hour later,

Whiskey made his way upstairs to find Kat sitting beside Ace's bed, reading a computer technology magazine to him. He chuckled, shaking his head at the scene. Another brother and he'd be jealous, but not Ace.

Across the hall, he saw Zulu reading a book. He tapped on the door frame, and Zulu looked up and nodded.

"Hey, man, come on in. Not like I can stop you. Doc won't let me close the door for another day or so," he smiled.

"Just trying to make sure you're okay, brother. You are okay, aren't you?" asked Whiskey. "That son-of-a-bitch was a huge piece of animal."

"All good, man. Really, I'm feeling better, although I'm going to start thinking of some new ways to train in case I run up against any more Dolfs." Whiskey laughed and stood to leave.

"Oh, by the way, Hawk said you had a message on the restaurant line. Someone named Gabi said she needed your help but hung up before he could ask about it."

"Gabi?" he said, scrunching his face. "Don't know anyone named Gabi. Not ringing a bell at all. That's odd."

"Oh, well, she'll call back if she needs us. Sleep good, man," he said, moving back across the hall. "Hey, baby girl, what do you say we get some sleep? You good, Ace?" Ace nodded, a small smile slipping from his lips. He raised a hand toward Whiskey, and Whiskey could only stare for a moment. Slowly reaching out, he gripped his brother's hand and smiled.

"Thank you, Ace. Thank you for helping to save my girl," he said, squeezing his hand. Ace dropped his hand quickly, but it was enough that Whiskey had a tear in his eye. Ace nodded and closed his eyes. Taking Kat's hand, he led her to their room and locked the door.

"After Christmas, we go to my house, baby. I know there's a lot happening for the holiday, so we'll stay here for now, but when it's done, we're home."

"That sounds perfect, Wade," she said, hugging him. "Will you make love to me, Wade? Will you hold me and make love to me tonight?"

"Tonight, and every night, baby girl. Forever."

CHAPTER THIRTY-FOUR

As Christmas dawned over their small mountain community, the snow glistening on the ground beneath a bright blue sky. The smells of holiday baking and cooking filled the barn. The men slowly made their way to the club, those staying already downstairs enjoying George's Christmas breakfast of cinnamon rolls, eggs, bacon, and pancakes.

Kat could hardly contain her excitement for the gifts beneath the tree. She'd gone a bit overboard, but she needed to do something good with her money, and she knew in her heart this was it. Her only concern was how everyone would react. On one hand, they might all see it for what it was, generosity to others. On the other, they might feel uncomfortable and being unable to give her something of equal value. It was a huge risk, but something she'd discussed in private with Bree, who encouraged her to follow her heart.

"Alright, everyone, let's go into the big room and open gifts," said Grace, pushing everyone out of the kitchen. In years past, the guys didn't really exchange gifts. They would have a meal with one another, maybe buy something for a brother in need. But never in all their years did they go all out like this.

Most of the guys sat on the floor, while the ladies took the big comfortable seats in front of the fire by the tree. Grace and Ghost received a lot of baby gifts, except for the ruby and diamond necklace he gave to Grace, and her gift to him was a custom pair of leather motorcycle boots.

Doc gave Bree several pieces of jewelry, and she returned the favor, giving him a very expensive watch.

Whiskey handed Kat her gift, and she gasped when she opened the small box.

"We got married so quickly, baby girl. We didn't have time to get rings. I hope you like them, but if you don't, we can get something different." She stifled the cries that she felt rumbling in her chest. The beautiful two-carat diamond with matching diamond band gleamed back at her.

"It's stunning, Whiskey. Absolutely stunning. I love it," she said, sliding them on her finger. "Thank you. I love you."

"Love you, baby girl," he said, smiling. Ace was seated next to her, and he smiled at their show of affection. Zulu was seated across from them, finally feeling a bit more like himself.

"Okay, my turn," Kat said, jumping up excitedly clapping her hands.

"What did you do, baby girl?" asked Whiskey, eyeing the woman, her excitement telling him that this was going to be uncomfortable.

"Hush. Okay, you know that my inheritance was... large, and, well, I don't really want it. I mean, we all know how I got it, and it wasn't exactly old-fashioned hard work. So, a large portion I designated for Isabella's House, as you all know."

"We know that, Kat," said Zulu. "What are you trying to say?"

"I wanted to do something for each of you. Something unique. Something you can't return." She stood and, from a black velvet bag, pulled out a bunch of envelopes. "George? I found out that you weren't able to afford a headstone for Margaret, so I had one made especially for her. There's a photo of it in there."

George opened the envelope and pulled out the picture. It was an angel, her arms crossed, looking downward. The huge pedestal must have been ten feet high. The headstone read 'For my Loving wife, Margaret. I Will Love You Always, George'.

"Oh, Sunshine," said George in a cracking voice, "you shouldn't have. You…"

"I should have, George. You and Margaret both deserve it. She's an angel looking down on all of us, your misguided children," she laughed. The others chuckled with her, and George hugged her close, clinging to the photo.

"Razor, Skull, Blade? I've been to museums all over the world. I've seen some of the great paintings and fine art that the masters gave us. The work you guys do in the garage is so amazing. It's artwork at its finest. It should be displayed like artwork." She handed them the envelopes.

"Holy fuck," whispered Razor. "She's expanding the garage and giving us a showroom. A full-on fucking showroom."

"And she's secured a spot for us at Sturgis next year to show the bikes," said Skull, "holy fucking hell, Kat." They all stood and hugged her, and she smiled, feeling the joy of giving.

"Zulu, Hawk, Gunner, and Eagle? I overheard you guys talking about needing more space to train. Soooo…" She handed off the envelopes.

"Son-of-a-bitch," said Gunner. "She's building a gym and range at the end of the road. It will be off-property but owned by Steel Patriots and can be opened to the public if we want, more revenue. The gym will be a training facility for MMA fighters. Colin has agreed to guest train." She nodded, smiling.

"Damn girl," said Zulu, welling up with tears. He pulled her tight and hugged her, kissing the top of her head.

"Ace? How could I forget about you, Ace? I know you like I know me." He nodded at her, still unable to speak without painful effort. "Your computer room is your sanctuary, and the more work that comes in, the more tools you'll need. Reading all those tech magazines to you this last week was informative." She handed him the envelope. He opened it and tried to speak but couldn't. Doc took the paper and read it.

"Two hundred and fifty thousand dollars designated to create a comms castle," he said, smiling. Ace nodded at her, and she smiled back.

"Tango, Ice, Axe? I learned that you all have siblings who have a disability." Again, she handed out the envelopes.

"Jesus, Kat," whispered Tango. "Two hundred and fifty thousand to my family to create an ideal environment for my sister and the same to the National Autism Foundation."

"Christ, same here," said Ice. "It's to the Downs' Syndrome Foundation in my brother's name."

"Juvenile Diabetes Foundation," said Axe, swallowing. "Thank you, Kat. Seriously, thank you."

"Doc and Bree," she said, smiling, "You welcomed me with open arms, love, and support. I've made some calls, and with Vincent's help, the licenses are secure. I'm building that clinic for us. There will be enough room for Bree to practice on one side and Doc on the other. Dr. Mullins from town is retiring but will be the physician of record."

"A... a clinic," said Doc. "You're giving me a fucking clinic... us a fucking clinic?"

"I am, for everyone," she said, smiling. Doc held her tightly, and then Bree hugged her, crying.

"Okay," she said with a big sigh, "Ghost and Grace, I know you built your dream home, so you don't need a home. I've already told you we'll use the Chesapeake house as a retreat or summer house for anyone who wants to use it. But I learned something very disturbing." Ghost frowned, looking at Grace and back at Kat.

"The two of you never got a honeymoon. So, I'm sending you on a European vacation for three weeks. We'll handle everything here. You can go now or after the baby is born, up to you. You'll go to London, Ireland, visit Ian," she said with a wink, "and then Italy, Greece, and then home."

"Oh, my God," said Grace, "that's... that's the same tour the girls were taking. How did you know?"

"I have skills of my own," she said, smiling at Grace.

"Oh, Kat. Kat, this is the perfect... oh thank you!" she said, hugging the younger woman.

"Kat, that's so generous of you," said Ghost. "Thank you."

"Okay, last but not least, my husband," she said, smiling at him. She knew Whiskey was probably squirming in his seat, not wanting a gift like this. She knew that she risked even offending him by giving him anything worth so much money. But she also knew that she needed to give him something that would both show him how much she loved him, and also how little she wanted the money.

"I see your wheels turning, Whiskey." The room let out a low chuckle, and Whiskey just glared at them all. "Whiskey, my husband, my true love. I know what drove you out of the military, and I know how difficult that was for you. Your nature is to protect... to love... so I'm giving that gift to the world. There will be four schools built for girls in the war-torn areas you served in. They will be guarded, gated, and provide education for any child who wants to attend. They will be known as the W. English School of Freedom."

Whiskey opened his mouth to speak, and nothing came out. Never in a million years did he expect this as his gift. Never. He'd watched those poor schoolgirls die because the school they were kidnapped from couldn't provide protection for them. She was offering that now to more than four hundred girls around the globe. How fucking incredible?

"Baby girl, I... I don't know what to say," he croaked.

"You don't have to say anything, Whiskey. I love you so much. I love all of you so much. You've given me a family. Something I never had. I didn't want this money, but I can serve a greater purpose by using it for good, by giving it to good causes that I know will change the world. Thank you. Thank you all of you for allowing me to do this."

Whiskey grabbed her, pulling her closely to his chest, hugging her. She was the most amazing woman he'd ever met.

"I love you, baby girl," he whispered.

"Alright, alright," said George, wiping his eyes, "enough of this. It's time for dinner!" On cue, Vincent walked in with an armload of gifts as well, shaking hands and hugging each one of the team. Several hours later, they were all seated around the massive stone fireplace singing Christmas carols. Whiskey held Kat on his lap, the quilt wrapped around her legs.

"You did good today, baby girl. You changed a lot of lives with your gifts," he said.

"They changed my life. You changed my life, Whiskey. This? This is only the beginning. We're going to make sure we support all the things that need our support. We're going to give people a second chance when they need one." He nodded as she stood. "I'm headed up to bed. Don't rush. Enjoy the time with your brothers."

"Good night, everyone. Merry Christmas," she said. A chorus of good nights flew by her as Bree and Grace joined her, headed to their rooms.

The men stayed down for another hour, drinking and talking about past Christmases and how different this one was. Each of the men talked about their gift from Kat and how it would change their world and those around them. She'd truly done what her father would have wanted.

As Whiskey crawled into bed, he stared at the flickering star out the bedroom window, sending a silent prayer and thank you for the gift of Kat. And somewhere, he knew that twelve little girls were smiling at the new schools helping other girls just like them. It was a great Christmas indeed.

CHAPTER THIRTY-FIVE

New Year's Eve at the club was a crazy event. A live band played while couples danced and swayed across the floor, filled with champagne or the cocktail of their choice. Doc surprised Bree with a three-day weekend in Miami, enjoying some well-deserved fun in the sun away from all the chaos.

Whiskey looked across the table at Zulu and frowned. His friend looked completely worn out and exhausted. He was worried about him and had encouraged him once again to speak to Bree about his dreams.

"Another dream last night?" asked Whiskey. Zulu looked up at his friend and nodded.

"They're getting more vivid. More intense, if that makes sense. It's like I can smell her. I can feel her touching my skin, and then she's gone. I feel like I'm losing my fucking my mind, Whiskey. You know this isn't me, brother!"

"I know, man. I know. You gotta get some relief, brother." Zulu nodded again, looking up to see Ice walking toward him. He had gate duty tonight, and only cars with invitations got into the holiday party.

"What's up, man?" asked Zulu.

"Car at the gate says they need your help. Says her name is Gabi," said Ice. "She looks fucked up, brother, like she's been hit."

"Fuck and Doc's not here," said Zulu. "Whiskey? Come with?" Whiskey nodded, kissing Kat on the cheek and telling her he'd be back for her. Zulu walked into the cold night toward the car at the gate. A woman behind the wheel looked up at him. He couldn't see her very well in the dark but knew her face was marked and swollen.

"I'm Zulu," he said, ducking down. "Can I help you?"

"I... I'm in pain... please, can you help me... I'm Gabi." Zulu still had no idea who she was, but he let her pull through and then watched as she struggled to stand getting out of the car. Zulu easily lifted her in his arms. She wasn't heavy at all. Her curves fitting perfectly against his hard planes. Walking through the secured gate leading to their private entrance, he took the woman through and upstairs to the medical room. He sure as fuck wished Doc were here, but Whiskey was a crack medic as well.

Lying her down on the table, white-blonde hair spilled from the hoodie, her glowing eyes staring up at him. He gasped. It was her.

"You... you're her. You're the woman," he couldn't finish the sentence. What was he supposed to say? Hi, creepy guy here. I see you in my dreams.

Her hood slipped off, revealing silvery white-blonde hair, her skin almost ghost-like, but it was her eyes that had him transfixed. The translucent gray orbs stared back at him like swirling waves in the ocean. He could swear they were literally moving before his eyes.

Staring into his face, Gabi let out a sigh of relief. He was here, and he was exactly as she remembered. The problem was, she didn't think he remembered her.

"Do you remember me?" she said with a tight mouth.

"I'm trying. I mean, I see you sometimes and..." She shook her head.

"You were in Walter Reed for a bullet to the abdomen. I was your attending." The dawn of remembrance started to flow through him. "There was a storm, a hurricane, and most of the staff moved with the patients to higher floors, but you couldn't be moved. I stayed," she winced in pain.

"What's wrong? Where are you hurt?" he asked quickly.

"Everywhere," she moaned.

"What do you need me to do?" he said, staring down at her gorgeous eyes. She gripped his forearms and looked from him to Whiskey.

"For starters, I need you to put my jaw back in place, and then, after that, I need you to kiss me like you did in the hospital."

Happy fucking new year...

OTHER BOOKS BY MARY KENNEDY YOU

MIGHT ENJOY!

REAPER Security Series
Erin's' Hero
Lauren's Warrior
Lena's' Mountain
Sara's' Chance
Mary's Angel
Kari's Gargoyle
Rachelle's Savior
Adele's Heart
Tori's' Secret
Finding Lily
Montana Rules
Savannah Rain
Gray Skies
My First Choice
Three Wishes
Second Chances
One Day at a Time
When You Least Expect It
Missing Hearts
Trail of Love

My SEAL Boys (connections to the REAPER Series)
Ian
Noa
Carter
Lars
Trevor
Fitz
Chris
O'Hara

Strange Gifts Series
Dark Visions
Dark Medicine
Dark Flame

Steel Patriots MC Series
Ghost – Book One
Doc – Book Two

ABOUT THE AUTHOR

Mary Kennedy is the mother of two adult children, has an amazing son-in-law, and is grandmother to two beautiful grandsons. She works full-time at a job she loves, and writing is her creative outlet. She lives in Texas and enjoys traveling, reading, and cooking. Her passion for assisting veterans and veteran causes comes from a strong military family background. Mary loves to hear from her readers and encourages them to join her mailing list, as she'll keep you up-to-date on new releases at https://insatiableink.squarespace.com. You can also join her Facebook page at Insatiable Ink.

Dear Readers,

I love hearing from you and encourage you to visit my website Insatiable Ink. Leave me know your thoughts and ideas on new books or expanding on characters. It's also a safe space to give your own feelings, like those of the characters. I love reading about how you relate to the stories because as we all know, there's a little of each of them within us.

I look forward to hearing from you and hope you enjoy other books in my collections.

Explore... and enjoy!